LEVI BARBER

A Shiny Place to Die

First edition

Proofreading by Danielle Botz

This book was professionally typeset on Reedsy.
Find out more at reedsy.com

To my kids—Lucy, Jax, Colt, and Lea:
Be stubborn. Ask questions. Push for what you want and what you
know is right, even when it's uncomfortable or scary. Don't let
anyone tell you who you're supposed to be. I love you more than
anything, even when you're loud, chaotic, and testing my fucking
last nerve. You're the reason I keep showing up.

To the woman I love:
You saved me from myself. You brought peace where there was
chaos and pulled me out of a dark place without asking me to be
anyone else

Chapter 1

Mason had the gun in his mouth when God finally spoke.

The emergency alert tone sounded from his busted phone—one last notification before he bullet-fucked his skull. A cigar box rattled with the vibration on the upside-down milk crate he used as a nightstand. Roaches scattered from empty beer cans as the harsh light from the phone's grimy screen lit up the darkness.

His shoulders fell as he sighed around the barrel and pulled it out, stringing spit from steel to lip.

"Really?" he said to nobody. "Fuck me."

On the wall in front of him, peeling paint hid beneath posters of pixelated heroes, spaceships frozen mid-battle, and masked warriors standing on mountains of skulls. Every one of them had the same look: chin down, eyes up—ready to wreck something important.

Mason looked nothing like them. He was skinny and 5'8" with boots on. His hair was short and messy; his face was pale with dark sunken eyes. He looked like a crack fiend who spent too many nights on the streets. If he was honest, he looked like the guy who befriended the super villain but received neither friendship nor respect out of the deal.

The alert banner swallowed his lock screen.

EMERGENCY ALERT–NATIONAL Stay indoors. Unknown hostile entities reported in multiple major cities. Avoid open areas. Shelter in place. This is not a test.

Since when did they call protesters *hostile entities*?

The words blurred as he read them. His heart raced. Was it fear? Most likely, it was the line of coke he'd snorted earlier. It was his last celebration before it all went dark.

Outside, something screamed—or was it a wail? It sounded strange. It wasn't a car alarm, or a drunk neighbor. Definitely not a siren. It was feral. It sounded big. The scream sounded both far away and way too close.

He heard it echo down the alley; the sound bouncing off brick and broken glass. For a moment, the whole building held its breath. There was no arguing, no bass thumping through the walls, no toilets flushing in the plumbing above him. Just that sound lingering in the air like burned hair.

Mason's eyes flicked from the phone to the gun.

"So," he said, "you're sending BLM riots before I off myself. Cute, motherfucker."

He lowered the pistol into his lap, scraping his tongue on his upper teeth trying to remove the flavor of metal and oil from his mouth. Gun in-hand, he bounced it twice before he sat it on the bed beside him. The mattress sagged, a stained twin pressed straight onto the floor. The springs complained louder than he did.

Disappointed, Mason leaned back against the plaster, wiped his eyes and nose, and breathed deeply.

His eyes scanned the shit-hole apartment when a small roach climbed up the bedside and onto his pistol. The insect stopped on the handle and looked as though the warmth left behind from

Mason's grip had comforted the bug. Mason stared, unable to draw a difference between himself and the roach. Small and hated, diseased but alive. Mason crept his hand toward the insect, and the bug turned to face him. Mason didn't want to say it, but the idea made him pause.

"You and I are one and the same, little bunk mate."

A second alert popped up, then a third.

Stay inside. Do not engage.

He snorted. The roach scattered into the darkness where the mattress met the wall.

"Yep, I'm still high," he moaned.

He stood, bones popping, and shuffled to face the wall. The posters stared back at him, all these impossible men with no fear, no taxes, no overdue rent. He'd read all their stories. He watched all their sequels, and played all the games. None of them ever opened with the hero crying in a studio apartment that smelled like old sweat and chemical cleaner.

All those heroes lived and died for a purpose he hadn't found.

Mason was dealt a shitty hand from birth. And every card he'd drawn after only made things worse. His parents were trash. They made him trash. His childhood was one awful experience after another. As a teenager, he was in and out of juvie. All the while, no one gave a shit.

By the time he was an adult—when he was the one in charge—he found himself in a prison yard, doing slow circles while trying not to lose his mind. In those ten years, his only choice had been to tie himself to a group of men who thought hate was a religion. He never believed it. Where was this white power as his father nodded off with a needle in his arm? Or when his mother passed out on the couch with a bottle still in hand while the TV preached prosperity to an empty room? Where was this Aryan nation pride as he sat in this crumbling apartment, suicidal and alone? It was all bullshit.

But it didn't matter. Because now he was marked. And still, no one gave a shit. Not his old gang, not his new crew. And now, not even Mason.

He was jolted from his thoughts by a distant explosion. In the glossy poster in front of him, he saw his faint reflection: a space soldier, outnumbered and fighting back against all odds, defying death.

Not Mason, though. He'd decided tonight: bow out quietly. No more hoping for some heroic second act. There were no redemption arcs for guys like him.

Mason sneered at the poster then and turned toward the source of the sound.

The window rattled. Trash cans toppled outside—heavy things slamming into metal. A car horn blared, then cut off mid-wail. Someone screamed for help, the word chopped short as if God himself had pressed the mute button.

That's not a riot, he thought.

The thumping in Mason's chest picked up speed—a feeling he rarely got without the help of drugs or burying his face in a prostitute's tits.

He stepped toward the window and pressed his face against the streaked glass. What the fuck was going on out there?

Chaos—as he'd expected. A handful of people fleeing in all directions. Cars in the street below resembled a failed game of Tetris.

In the distance, a figure moved toward the panicked herd. He pressed his face harder into the glass, but it was hard to tell exactly what he was seeing.

As the thing got closer, it made even less sense. The joints weren't natural. Its limbs connected at angles that didn't compute in his brain. It maneuvered like a creature out of a sci-fi movie. How was it moving so quickly on those fucked-up crippled legs?

Outside, the sky growled. Deep thunder with a migraine. Mason jumped back as the window flashed a vivid green.

His brow furrowed. His head snapped up. His mother had told him a thousand times as a kid that the end was coming. Before he realized she was full of shit, he'd spend way too many nights thinking he might not wake up the next day because some almighty god was going to come down and scoop everyone up. Funny it would happen now.

"If this is the Rapture," he said to the ceiling, "you're way off schedule."

And he was right on time. He reached for the gun again. Better to get this over with.

But as he lifted the gun to his mouth, the poster across from him caught the light and his attention. He stared at it for a second.

The nameless space soldier—battle armor scorched, visor blacked out—seemed to tilt, just slightly, as the phone's glow slid across the glossy surface. Mason blinked hard. The face plate shimmered.

He shot a sharp laugh through his nose. "Yep," he said, "I'm still high."

The soldier didn't move. Of course he didn't. It was ink and paper and cheap glue peeling at the corners. Mason knew that. But that didn't stop the voice.

You're really going to bitch out now? The world finally gets interesting, and you're gonna miss it?

Mason scrubbed his face with the back of both hands. When

he looked again, the poster was the same as it had always been—frozen mid-battle, gun raised, fearless. Judging him by default.

"Who the fuck asked you?" Mason said aloud.

The words came anyway. Not sound—thought. They were mean in a way only he knew how to be to himself.

Funny how the world picked tonight to steal your spotlight. Go on. Pull the trigger.

His jaw tightened.

"What the fuck is that supposed to mean?" he snapped, pacing once, then stopping. His heart was pounding too fast. Coke and fear and the building shaking all blurred together.

It means no one noticed you when you were alive. And they won't notice you when you're dead either.

He swallowed.

"It's not about being noticed," he said, though the words tasted thin. He wiped his nose on his sleeve, angry at the tremor in his hands.

Sure, it isn't. You planned this whole thing like it mattered. Truth is, you wouldn't last two seconds out there, anyway. Look at you— shaking in your own apartment. Sniveling and crying like a little bitch because life is just too hard.

The poster's visor reflected his shape back at him. Pale. Skinny. Eyes blown wide and wet.

You're not a hero. You're a body waiting to happen. A statistic with a name nobody's gonna read.

"Fuck you," Mason said, louder now. He pointed at the wall like the soldier could hear him. "You don't know shit about me."

The thought came back immediately, cruel and calm.

I know this ending fits. You came in as nothing. You'll go out the same.

Mason's face got hot. The sonofabitch was right. If he pulled the trigger now—right now—it wouldn't be *his* ending anymore. It'd just be another casualty in the pile. His death wouldn't matter—just like the rest of his existence hadn't mattered.

And that—more than his life, more than the gun in his hand—made a hot and ugly feeling flare in his chest.

Pistol in-hand, he opened the box on his busted milk crate. His life's remnants were inside: a half-pack of smokes, a weed-ash-covered lighter, a bag of twenties from his last job, and some loose 9 mm rounds.

He checked the magazine; almost empty. He loaded the few rounds into it, then slapped it back in with the easy muscle memory you didn't put on a resume.

Next came the knife—a thick, ugly KA Bar knock-off with a chipped tip and a shitty, hollow handle. The knife was more gimmick than tool. He slipped it into the waistband of his jeans, under the oversized hoodie that once had a white-power logo across the chest. He'd blacked most of it out with Sharpie, but you could still see the outline if you looked long enough.

Maybe he could fix at least one mistake tonight.

He jammed his bare feet into his boots without untying them. The building shook again, dust raining from the ceiling as a mass hit somewhere close. A woman shrieked in the hallway; a man shouted for her to shut her fucking mouth.

The phone buzzed with another alert. He didn't bother reading it this time.

"Hey," he rasped, looking up at the cracked ceiling. "If you're doing this, don't half-ass it. Full send the shitstorm, big guy."

No answer, unless you counted the distant boom of structures collapsing.

Mason swallowed, faced the exit, and opened the door.

Chapter 2

The hallway smelled like wet paint and microwaved noodles. Flickering fluorescents stuttered overhead, turning everything into a stop-motion nightmare. Apartment doors were cracked open; faces peered out, eyes wide and unhelpful.

On the second-floor landing, a guy in a tank top stood in his doorway, puffing his chest out so far it looked painful. He held a Louisville Slugger with a death grip, but the tip of the bat wouldn't stop shivering in the air. He was doing his best 'man of the house' impression, but Mason could see the sweat slicking his neck.

"What's going on?" the guy asked.

Mason shrugged. "End of the world and you're next at bat, Slugger."

The man blinked. "We're supposed to stay inside, Dipshit."

"…fuck you just say to me?" Mason asked, rolling the gun in his wrist, not missing a step.

The man shrank backwards and closed the door without a word.

At the ground level, the front door glass was already spider-webbed with cracks. Dark streaks smeared down the handle.

Outside, sirens played a broken harmony with screams and distant gunfire. The stench of hot metal and fear saturated the air around him.

This was insane. He should have been terrified. And to his surprise, he wasn't. The thing he'd feared most was already coming— he'd made the choice to die. The rest of this was just bonus time.

He kicked the door open. His poorly tied boot laces slapped the rustic leather of the boots and slim fitted tattered denim jeans as he broke forth—chest out and ready to face the death waiting on the other side.

The street looked like somebody had shaken the city and all the loose parts fell out. Cars sat at stupid angles, doors hanging open, alarms blaring. One lay on its side, wheels still spinning, glass glittering across the asphalt. A fire hydrant sprayed water into the air in a wild silver arc, mixing with gasoline and making a rainbow in the gutters.

And in the middle of it all, there it was. The thing looked like somebody fucked a greyhound and a rat, then hit randomize on the offspring. Long limbs, joints crooked, skin like wet leather stretched over lean muscle that twitched on its own. Its head was mostly jaw and teeth, glistening as it snapped at a shape on the ground.

For a moment, Mason thought it had a man. Then he realized it was ripping at a dress.

The woman inside the dress was screaming and kicking, hands clamped on the creature's neck just below the jaw— must've been the only thing anchoring her to life. She wore what was left of a nightclub outfit—sparkling silver fabric torn at the thigh, shoes missing, hair wild.

Two other creatures crouched nearby, snarling at each other

as they grabbed at the glittering strips of cloth and jewelry. They yanked, each pulling a bit of shine toward themselves like toddlers fighting over a toy. Their eyes—entrenched, reflective, insect-dark—were locked not on the woman, but on the things that sparkled.

A cold, manic spark ignited behind his eyes. They liked shiny shit.

Just like us, he thought.

He raised the gun out of habit more than hope.

"Okay," he muttered, eyes rolling up briefly. "Here's your chance to walk me back from the ledge. You screw this up, this one's on you."

He sighted on the nearest creature—the one ripping at the lower part of the dress.

The first shot ripped through the air like a physical blow. The bullet took the thing square in the side of its elongated skull. Its head snapped sideways in a spray of dark, viscous blood that glowed faintly when it caught the streetlight. The creature lurched and collapsed like somebody had unplugged it.

The woman shrieked louder.

The other two beasts froze, limbs tensing, then whipped their heads toward him, eyes flaring like a possum's eyes in moonlight. For a heartbeat, nobody moved—just the hiss of water from the broken hydrant cascading in the distance and the echo of the gunshot.

One down. A rush of something—excitement maybe— flooded his body.

He nodded toward them. "Ha! Surprise, ya fucking cunts," he taunted.

They came at him simultaneously, fast and strange. It was like they'd never seen gravity or asphalt before. Mason squeezed again. The second shot shattered one's front leg; the thing face-planted over itself, careening across the asphalt in a smear of claws and teeth.

The third one went wide, smashing the window of a parked car. Glass erupted and fell like diamonds. Both creatures' heads snapped to the falling shards.

They stared as the glass rained down, a chorus of soft clinks creating a twisted lullaby. For half a second, they seemed to forget the gun, the woman—everything. They pawed at the ground, fighting over who got more pieces of broken windshield.

A grizzled laugh escaped him. What the fuck?

The uninjured one darted for a chunk of chrome bumper instead of him. Mason stepped forward and put the third round into the base of its neck. The beast convulsed, twitched, and lay still.

The wounded one hissed, torn leg dragging, face dropping to the ground every time it put weight on the mangled leg. It crawled toward a little cascade of glass sliding off the car seat onto the street.

Shit. Mason realized his magazine was almost dry.

That was fine. He'd have to do this another way. He put the gun in his waistband, swapping it for the crude blade.

The creature was bigger up close, easily the size of a Great Dane—tendons and muscle flexing eerily under hairless skin. As it wrapped a hand—or whatever the fuck those things were— around a glittering shard, Mason brought the knife down into the underside of its throat. He grasped the thin skin on the back of the creature's head. The blade hit cartilage and dragged on for an uncomfortable moment as he sawed at the beast's throat before it finally popped through.

The alien jerked, claws scraping against his arm as its blood poured hot over his fingers. It snapped at him in reflex but missed by inches. He grabbed its jaw with his free hand and shoved it away while he slashed the knife sideways, ripping through something that felt like garden hose and gristle.

He was breathing hard from the effort by the time the creature stopped moving.

His heart pounded in his ears, and for the first time in a long time, *he felt it*—that hollow, black pit in his chest filling with something sharp and electric. Not happiness. Not peace. Something exhilarating.

Fire roared in his gut. He looked down at his hands. They trembled, slick with dark blood that smelled like rust and pennies and the stale vulgarity of piss. His body screamed that he was alive. His brain screamed that this was insane. Somewhere in between, something smiled.

The woman on the ground scrambled backward. Her eyes were wide, pupils huge in the streetlight.

He finally got a good look at her—mixed features, high cheekbones, dark curls streaked with sweat and whatever passed for alien gore, skin that somehow looked beautiful even under the sodium-orange glow of the streetlamp. One strap of her glittering dress hung useless. She was bare foot, toenails painted white. She looked like someone had dropped a nightclub angel into a horror movie.

"Hey," Mason said, chest heaving. "You good?"

She stared past him. "Behind you," she said—her voice low and even.

The world narrowed.

He spun.

Another one, smaller but faster, leaped from the roof of a

parked sedan, aiming straight for Mason's face. Claws spread, teeth bared, eyes fixated not on him, but on the metal ring on his finger—a cheap band he'd stole from the chink market downtown, scratched and bright in the street lamps.

He didn't have time for the gun.

Mason froze, all that bad ass fury was gone. The shittier man inside him must have decided it was time to show up again. He held his knife hand low. The thing's lower legs hit him chest-first; the two went down hard together. His shoulder hit pavement. The creature shrieked directly in his ear, paws reaching up Mason's left arm. Claws dug into his hoodie. He fell to his back. The creature pawed and pried at the shiny trinket ring. As he tried to hide it with his other hand, the monster let out a gurgled howl. Mason raised his head out of the fetal position and returned the creatures scream, desperately pushing out all the air he had left inside him. He slammed the knife upward, into its ribs, and kept going until he felt resistance. With his off hand, he grabbed a handful of whatever meat he could find, shoved, and twisted.

He drove his knee up, rolled, and used the thing's own weight to slam its head into the curb.

The shriek cut off with a wet crunch.

Silence crashed down over the street, broken only by distant sirens and his own ragged breathing.

Mason stayed there on his hands and knees, panting and coughing up years of gunk and shit left behind by weed and cigarettes. The knife was still buried in alien's rib cage. The dark pit inside his stomach—fear, loneliness, all the girls he fucked and bailed on, all his greedy and misaligned morals, his low self esteem, and his shitty attitude now blazed like somebody had poured gasoline into his gut and lit a match.

He pulled the knife free and stood sweaty and wobbling.

Behind him, the woman was pulling herself upright, wincing as she put weight on one ankle. Her dress glittered in jagged strips, catching every stray beam of light like a signal flare.

"Stay down," he hissed, but his warning came too late.

Headlights swung across them as a car tried to reverse away from something further up the street. The beams caught her, turning the sequins into a maelstrom of white stars.

Mason watched her glow and thought: *If I wanted to bait these things, I'd use this dumb bitch.*

He didn't have to wait long to be proven right.

A growl rolled down the block. Not one, but many. Shadows moved on rooftops, in alleys, and between the gaps in panic-stopped traffic. Eyes winked into existence like someone had poked holes in the dark and filled them with reflected light.

The woman swallowed.

"Okay," she said softly. "Show's over. Time to go."

"Go where?" he snapped, voice sharp with adrenaline. "These things are fucking everywhere."

"Anywhere but right here seems like a solid fucking plan," she said, gesturing for him to move.

Another growl, closer now.

He scanned the area for cover: dumpsters, cars, and storefronts. Most had glass walls, all of which were an all-you-can-eat buffet of shiny. One big green dumpster lay on its side halfway down the alley between his building and the next. The lid was cracked open—an invitation.

"Come on," she said, grabbing his wrist and pulling him along with her. "Trash day."

He protested at first. Then, his watery eyes flicked to the shadows and back. He drew in a deep breath.

The two of them hobbled over to the container. His left leg was throbbing; he only now noticed the wet warmth soaking through his jeans. In the chaos, — a claw or a tooth —something had opened him up.

As they reached the dumpster, something slammed into a car behind them. The vehicle rocked on its shocks. Glass shattered. Gleaming fragments fountained into the air, and the chorus of growls behind them twisted into a hungry frenzy.

Chapter 3

Mason dove first, shoulder smashing into plastic trash bags. The smell of rot and sour beer exploded around him. The woman scrambled in after him, and let the lid fall closed just as something heavy clipped the side, sending a metallic clang reverberating through the dark interior.

Inside the overturned dumpster, it was cramped and rank and weirdly intimate. Mason lay on his back, staring up at the stained metal above them, chest heaving. He could hear claws scratching on asphalt outside, bodies slamming into cars, and distant screams chopped short.

His leg burned. When he reached down, his fingers came up wet and sticky.

"Don't," he started as she shifted beside him.

She ignored him and felt down his pant leg. Her fingers were warm and steady as they found the tear and the blood. He couldn't remember the last time someone touched him in a nurturing way. He resisted the urge to swat her hand away.

"Shit," she muttered. "Through and through."

"Through and through?" he asked. "What's that mean?" It sounded obvious, but Mason needed confirmation. She offered no reply.

"Hey." His voice was raspy. She couldn't just say shit like that and then go quiet. "Through and through what!?"

He tried to push her hands away. She slapped his wrist aside like she was swatting a bug.

"Hold still," she said without pulling focus from his leg.

"No, you cunt. What's—"

That did it. She pounced on him. One arm snaked around his throat, and before he could process the shift in weight, she had him in a choke hold, his head slammed back against the cold, reeking metal.

Pain sparked behind his eyes. He squeezed them shut and tried to breathe.

"Listen to me," she hissed in his ear. "You helped me, but that doesn't give you a pass to say any out-of-pocket shit that comes to your fucked-up head. I'm trying to help you in return. Which is more and more difficult each time I look at the swastika on your hoodie that you did a piss-poor job of blacking out."

Mason's face tightened. He tried to explain with the little air he had.

"It's not—"

"I don't give a shit," she said. "You don't have to explain yourself to me. See? I'm not such a cunt after all." Her tone was sweet, which was somehow more terrifying. "But I can be if that's how you want to play this shit," she added.

He clawed at her forearm, more in reflex than in real resistance. How the fuck was she so strong? She wasn't big enough to be so strong.

"If you've got a problem with my survival plan," she said, voice steady despite the chaos outside, "you can file a complaint against my black ass later. Like, when we're not hiding in a trash can surrounded by alien crackheads."

He wheezed a laugh despite himself.

"Okay," he said. "Okay, okay. Ease up. I'm not a fucking Nazi."

"Right," she said. It was dark in the cramped space, but Mason could feel her eyes rolling as she said it.

"I'm fucking not. I'm not a boy scout either, though. I was in prison. Not a lot of options to stay safe…. I had… to pick," he said, gasping for air between words.

She held a beat longer, then released him. He sucked in air. His throat burned and his vision pulsed at the edges.

He blinked up at her. His throat now burned along with everything else.

"You military?" he asked, rubbing the outside of his neck where she'd held him. "Or just one of those freaky MMA bitches?"

"Ex-military," she said. "Tenth Mountain. Afghanistan."

"Figures," he muttered. "Should've known God would send a fucking infantry angel."

She smirked, bright white teeth peeking out for just a second. "Cute. You always talk this much when you're bleeding out?"

Another impact came from outside. The dumpster rocked, and the woman came crashing into him.

"Shit," she hissed, bringing her hands up quickly. "Did I hit your leg?"

Mason didn't answer. He was distracted by the smell of her. It was too familiar.

For half a second, he wasn't in a dumpster with a strange woman. He was in the small bathroom of a cheap duplex. His mom leaned against the sink. Her makeup was smeared, and a cigarette she'd already forgotten about burned down between her fingers.

The smells of smoke and cheap soap always cramped that

small space. It filled his nostrils as he sat and listened to his mom ramble on—always one empty promise after another. Then she'd hug him too tight and for too long. He'd carried that scent on him through so many disappointing days. How perfect that he smelled it again today.

Something slammed into the dumpster again, pulling him out of the memory. He jumped, but the woman didn't flinch. He knew he was fucked up. But what was wrong with her to be so unbothered in the middle of all this?

Sirens howled then burnt out somewhere distant, layered over the guttural screeches of the creatures or humans caught in the mix. Another something hit the lid hard enough to dent it inward by an inch. Mason pressed himself harder against the bottom of the dumpster.

"What's your name?" he asked, trying to distract himself.

"Rae," she said. "You?"

He thought about lying. It was the end of the world, and he was technically supposed to be dead by now. But instead, he went with the truth.

"Mason."

"Okay, Mason the ex-Nazi," Rae said, voice dropping into something calm and razor-sharp. That tone probably came in handy when she was trying to motivate soldiers to become bullet sponges. "Here's the situation. You've got a hole in your leg, we've got a city full of demon lizards with a jewelry fetish, and I have a friend at the club who needs my help."

"I've got nothing better to do," he said. "Might as well go clubbing, I guess."

"Great," she said. "Then let's get moving."

He stared at the rusted underside of the lid, listening to the chaos outside.

"So what's the plan, Major Pain?" he asked.

She shifted, peeking through a thin crack where the lid met the bent sidewall. Her eyes narrowed.

She jerked her chin toward the gap. "You see that Humvee up the street?"

He shifted carefully, leg burning, and peered through the same crack.

There it was, maybe a hundred yards away. A tan, light-armored Humvee sat sideways in the intersection. It looked like someone had tried to block the street before they abruptly stopped existing. Bodies in uniform lay slumped nearby, gear scattered—helmets, rifles, spent shell casings. Aside from the crack in the windshield, it looked mostly untouched.

Beside it, eight to ten alien corpses lay in broken heaps, riddled with bullet holes. About what he'd expect from government workers.

"I see it," Mason said.

Rae leaned back, her face exhausted but eyes sharp. "We get to that truck, we've got armor, weapons—maybe a radio. We can move. Sitting here, we're just takeout in a green box."

"Big assumption," he said. "You don't even know if the keys are in it."

She looked at him flatly. "Humvees don't have keys, Dumbass."

"Well, excuse the fuck out of me, G.I. Jane," Mason scoffed under his breath. How the fuck was he supposed to know that?

He thought for a second about the gun in his mouth earlier that night; about the poster heroes; about God timing the apocalypse right when he'd finally decided to suck-start a pistol. The fact that God seemed to want everyone dead now really pissed him off. It was enough to push him forward for a little longer, despite the shitshow this had become.

"Fuck it," he said. "Guess I don't have a better plan."

"Good," Rae said. "Because I'm not dying in a fucking dumpster."

Rae's hand found his shoulder, fingers digging in just enough to anchor him.

"On my count," she whispered. "We go."

Mason licked his dry lips and felt his pulse thud in his throat.

"Got anything you wanna say to the big guy before we sprint through the buffet line?" she asked.

Mason considered, eyes wide.

"Yeah." He placed his palms together and squeezed his eyes shut. "Dear Lord, let me run faster than this bitch."

Rae snorted and slapped his leg. "Don't bleed out and you may have a chance, Smartass."

Mason tried to cover his wince with a smirk.

"Ready," she said. "Three… two… one—"

She kicked the lid open. Neon light flooded the can—sickly streetlamp light and flashing red strobes poured into the dumpster. Cold air rushed over them. Mason scrambled after her, every nerve screaming as his wounded leg protested.

They'd tumbled out into a war zone. Their run to the Humvee wasn't graceful or strategic. It was more like two dipshits caught shoplifting during the apocalypse, who just realized the manager was a demon with too many teeth.

As they got closer, Rae sprinted—bare feet slapping asphalt, tattered dress fluttering like a flag, breath sharp and controlled. Mason limped after her, each step sending a lightning bolt of pain up his thigh. His vision flickered at the edges. The blood loss was catching up, but adrenaline shoved it back for now.

Behind them, creatures burst out like someone had flushed Hell's toilet. They skidded across the pavement, claws grinding down, heads jerking toward Rae as her mangled silver dress glittered in the streetlights.

"Shit—shit—*shit,*" Mason gasped, picking up speed he didn't actually have.

"Don't look back!" Rae yelled.

"Oh, profound idea, Rae!"

They reached the first parked car. Rae vaulted over the hood with the fluidity of a woman who had definitely done stupid things under fire before. Mason tried the same. His bad leg caught the wheel well. He rolled across the windshield instead, swearing loudly as glass cracked in spider-web gaps beneath him.

"Keep moving," Rae barked.

"I'm trying—"

Rae reached the Humvee first.

The surrounding bodies told the whole story: three National Guard soldiers, throats torn out, empty rifles near their hands—shell casings everywhere. They'd gone down hard and fast.

Rae didn't blink. She reached down and pulled a holstered Beretta from a soldier's corpse. Possibly the only weapon around them that might still have ammo.

She grabbed the Humvee's front door handle. It didn't budge.

"Come on, come on," she hissed, yanking at it.

Behind her, Mason skidded to a stop, raising his pistol with shaking hands. The nearest creature lunged. He fired twice—one round hit its shoulder; the other buried itself in the hood of a truck with a metallic clang.

The injured alien spun toward him with a hiss. Mason pulled the trigger again, but instead of firing, it only clicked. Fuck. It was dry.

"Oh, good," Mason said. "Now you're pissed." He flung the

empty pistol onto the asphalt ahead of him.

"Mason," Rae barked. "Move, fucker!"

He staggered to her side. Rae jerked at the door latch of the Humvee again. Once. Twice. It refused to open.

"Fucking Military issue bullshit! Are you shitting me?!" she screamed.

The other aliens were thirty yards away at that point and closing in fast. Their eyes flickered with reflected light. They moved like spastic dogs, skidding around on the pavement, their feet struggling to gain purchase.

Mason reached down and grabbed one of the fallen soldiers' rifles. Of course, it was empty. He threw it in the nearest alien's path like a baseball bat. Useless, but satisfying.

Rae, meanwhile, had run around the Humvee, yanking at the passenger door.

"What the fuck," Mason shouted.

The door swung open.

"Get in," she said. Her screams barely made it over the surrounding noise.

She dove in headfirst and slid into the driver's seat, reaching over and examining some switch he assumed made the thing actually fucking go.

The alien pack hit the driver's side of the vehicle while Mason moved around to the open passenger door.

The Humvee rocked sideways from the impact, pushing Mason back a few steps. One creature clawed at the driver's side mirror, another leaped onto the hood, teeth bared inches from the windshield. Its breath fogged the glass with steam and strings of spit.

"Jesus Christ," Mason yelled, grabbing the heavy door frame

and jumping in.

He slammed his door—or tried to.

The moment he pulled, another alien at full speed, body-slammed the open door.

The door snapped shut with the full weight of an armored vehicle behind it.

And Mason's left hand—his stupid, slow left hand—was still on the frame.

The door crushed down on his fingers like a guillotine.

He didn't scream at first. The pain didn't register immediately. Instinctively, he jerked his hand free from the door frame. Blood sprayed across the inside of the window. Something small and pale bounced off Rae's thigh as he whipped his hand back and forth in front of his face. He couldn't look away from the mess. It was like he needed confirmation that this was actually happening.

Three fingers—ring, middle, and index—were now nothing more than bloody stumps in the middle of his hand. He stared, taking in the reality for a second.

"GO—GO—DRIVE, DRIVE," he shrieked, clutching his mutilated hand.

Rae didn't hesitate. The Humvee roared to life.

She slammed it into drive, tires struggling to find motivation, and the aliens were thrown backwards as the transmission finally kicked into gear and the vehicle clambered down the trashed roadway.

One persistent creature with a shredded face shook off the hit and bounded after them, claws tearing chunks out of the pavement with each stride.

Rae's eyes were glued to the mirror. "Mason—pressure on your damn hand!"

He shook his head violently, eyes squeezed shut. "FUCK—FUCK—I'M,"

She grabbed his wrist with one hand, shoved his mangled fingers into a wad of cloth torn from her dress at her crotch, and forced his palm shut.

"Pressure," she said.

"Aaagh. Stop."

"Do it!"

"Jesus, I'm trying," he said. He did his best to apply pressure and keep his cool—whatever was left of it. Between the blood and the pain, it was all he could do not to puke all over the inside of the Humvee. He wanted to just pass out. How was he not in some kind of shock at this point? If this was how this apocalypse shit was going to go, he should have just shot himself when he had the chance.

Mason's head was pressed against the window as he watched Rae navigate the maze of wrecked cars and carnage.

"Where are we going?" he asked.

"I told you," she said, "I have to go get my friend."

"This isn't a playdate. We don't have time to go pick up friends. We need to get somewhere safe."

"I'm not leaving her behind," Rae said. "If you've got a problem with it, feel free to call an Uber."

"I never should have left the fucking club," she said to herself more than to him. "I never should have gone to the fucking club to start with."

Mason said nothing.

"Figures the one night I let her stick me in a stupid fucking dress and stupid fucking shoes, the whole goddamn world falls apart."

Rae gripped the steering wheel, her eyes locked forward. Mason kept quiet, not sure what to say. She had to know as well as he did that nothing good was going to be waiting at club full of lights and loud music.

Chapter 4

Rae slowed them a half-block out. She stopped the Humvee in front of the club and let out a deep sigh, her hands still clenching the steering wheel.

The club's front entrance yawned open, one door hanging crooked, bass still thumping faintly inside—looping, warped, like a heartbeat that didn't know it was dead yet. Neon leaked out in weak pinks and blues, flickering across broken glass.

Rae slipped inside, Baretta in-hand at the low-ready.

Mason watched her the way you watch someone defuse a bomb—quiet, careful, and ready for everything to go wrong.

She cleared the left, paused, then listened.

The air inside was thick with smoke, sweat, and something coppery underneath. Fog machines hissed intermittently, coughing clouds into a room full of corpses. Strobe lights flashed in uneven bursts, freezing the carnage into snapshots— bodies twisted on the dance floor, glitter smeared into blood, shattered mirrors catching light like bait.

Mason's stomach clenched. Rae glanced at the bodies as she moved.

A cluster of aliens crouched among the dead. Some pawed through jewelry, while others raked through glow sticks. The remaining handful gnawed at the bodies themselves. One dragged a mirrored tray across the floor, entranced by its own reflection.

The creatures hadn't noticed them…yet. Rae's jaw tightened. She stepped forward.

Mason saw it then—the body near the edge of the dance floor. A woman on her side, curls dark with blood, one heel still on, the other missing.

Rae's breathing hitched once. Then she raised the gun.

The first shot stunned Mason.

One creature's skull burst in a spray of black gore and glitter. The second spun, shrieked, and went down mid-lunge. Rae advanced as she fired—controlled, relentless—each muzzle flash strobing the room harder than the club lights ever had.

The creatures scrambled, shrieking, claws skidding on glass and blood. The muzzle flashes drew them in as Rae cut them down one by one. Her dress caught the light—silver and torn and glowing like a flare.

One of them collapsed sideways and kept moving anyway—legs churning against empty air, claws digging grooves into the ground as if momentum alone might carry it forward. Another spun hard, body jerking in sharp, broken motions, its limbs firing out of sequence, commands misfiring somewhere deep inside it.

Mason backed toward a pillar, heart pounding. "Rae—"

She didn't hear him.

She fired again. And again. Each shot was punctuated by snarls, bodies dropping, and the wet slap of each one hitting the floor. They didn't scream. They tried to run.

Muscle memory fought reality. Nerves kept shouting orders long after the bodies could obey. One creature dragged itself in a tight arc, scraping forward on its flank, eyes still locked on the line ahead, still convinced the charge wasn't over.

It came toward her, drawn by the shine and the noise. Rae sidestepped and put two rounds into its chest.

The low thump of the sound system and the death rattles of the dying creatures filled the room. Smoke curled from the barrel of her gun. Broken glass clinked as it settled to the floor.

Rae stood there breathing hard, gun still raised, eyes scanning until she was sure—absolutely sure—nothing else moved.

Then she lowered the Beretta. She walked to her friend and kneeled.

The rage drained out of her all at once, like someone had pulled a plug. She set the gun down carefully, hands suddenly shaking, and touched her friend's shoulder with two fingers.

"Hey," she whispered. "Hey… I'm here."

Mason stayed where he was.

Rae sat back on her heels, staring at the body. Her voice was stripped bare.

"I told her I needed air," she said. "The music was too loud. The lights—" She swallowed. "I don't do well when things get crowded. She knew that."

She pressed her lips together, breathing through her nose. In. Out. Like she was counting something only she could see.

"She dragged me out anyway," Rae continued. "Said I needed to loosen up. Said one drink wouldn't kill me."

A humorless huff escaped her.

"I never even wanted to go."

Mason limped closer but didn't interrupt.

"I should've stayed," Rae said. Not accusing. Just stating it. "I always leave early. Always find the exit."

Her hands clenched in her lap, then loosened. She didn't cry. She just… emptied.

She looked up at Mason finally. "Can you give me a minute?"

"Yeah," he said. "Take your time."

He turned away before she could see his face.

Mason limped toward the bar, each step tugging at the wet heat in his leg. The TVs overhead were still on, volume muted, emergency tickers crawling endlessly across the bottom of the screens.

MULTIPLE METROPOLITAN AREAS AFFECTED

Los Angeles–Chicago–Atlanta–New York

UNKNOWN ORIGIN ENTITIES DISPLAY ATTRACTION TO LIGHT AND REFLECTIVE SURFACES

He frowned. Another banner slid through.

POWER GRID REMAINS ACTIVE–OFFICIALS WARN OUTAGES IMMINENT. AVOID ILLUMINATED AREAS

"Yeah," Mason muttered. "That tracks."

He leaned on the bar, dizzy, watching footage loop—grainy helicopter shots, creatures swarming intersections, lights drawing them in like moths to a city-sized flame.

"Where the fuck did you even come from?" he whispered at the screen. "And why here?"

No answers.

Behind him, Rae stayed kneeling, head bowed, saying goodbye in silence.

Mason looked away and read the ticker again. While he watched, he reached across the bar to grab a bottle. The top shelf was wrecked, but the shitty stuff at the bottom remained intact. He poured himself a glass of something amber without reading it and sat and waited for Rae to snap back.

After several moments, Rae stood. She didn't look back at her friend again. Just rose, shoulders squaring, spine locking into place like she'd sealed something behind a door she'd learned to keep shut.

She walked to the bar. Mason watched her—watched the Beretta stay loose in her hand, muzzle down but ready. Watched the way her eyes kept moving, tracking reflections in mirrors, the dull glow of LEDs, the faint shimmer of broken glass underfoot.

She reached behind the bar, grabbed the first bottle her hand landed on, and didn't bother checking the label either.

Whiskey.

She twisted the cap off, found a chipped tumbler, and poured herself a drink that had no interest in being civilized. The smell hit Mason—sharp, burned, familiar.

She took it down in one pull.

Didn't cough. Didn't blink.

Rae slid onto a bar stool beside him, poured another finger, smaller this time, and finally exhaled.

Mason lifted his own glass.

"So," he said, voice low. "What's the next move?"

She didn't answer immediately.

He glanced around the club—at the bodies, the lights still pulsing weakly, the emergency broadcasts lying silently overhead.

"This is a decent place to die," he added. "At least we've got alcohol."

Rae snorted once: short and dry.

"No," she said. "We're not dying here."

She poured the rest of the whiskey into her glass and watched it slosh. "We're going to my brother's place."

Mason turned toward her. "Your brother."

"He's a paramedic," she said. "And ex-military. Keeps supplies at home. Trauma kits. Antibiotics. The good shit."

Her eyes flicked to his leg.

"And you're bleeding like a stuck pig."

Mason followed her gaze and grimaced. "Yeah. That tracks."

She pushed the glass toward him. "Drink."

He did.

"From what I can tell," Mason said, wiping his mouth, "these things are everywhere. Big cities got hit first. LA, Chicago, New York. Power's still on—for now—but the broadcasts are saying outages are coming. Creatures are drawn to light, shine, and reflections."

Rae nodded slowly. "That explains the club."

"And your dress," he added, softer.

She didn't look down at it.

"Also explains why we haven't been swarmed yet," he continued. "Humvee's matte. No glow. No sparkle."

A low, wet sound echoed from the dance floor.

Both of them froze. One of the creatures twitched—a final nerve firing—claws scraping weakly against glass before going still.

Rae watched it for a long moment.

"You gonna be okay?" Mason asked.

She picked up the whiskey.

Didn't answer right away.

Then she slammed the rest of it back, set the glass down hard enough to crack it, and stood.

"I'll be fine," she said evenly. No bravado. No promise. Just a statement she intended to make true.

She grabbed the Beretta, checked the chamber, then looked at Mason.

"Finish up," she said. "We're moving."

Mason drained his glass, winced as it burned down his throat, and slid off the stool.

"Guess we don't get to die classy after all," he muttered.

Rae headed for the door.

Outside, the Humvee waited. Behind them, the club lights flickered, then went dark.

They climbed into the Humvee, doors slamming shut just as a creature skittered in the alley nearby—too slow, too late.

Rae shifted the Humvee into drive.

Not far down the road, they came across a large pack of creatures. The entire group was feeding on bodies that lay scattered across the ground.

Rae swerved, hitting one of the larger beasts in the group. The sharp turn led the Humvee straight up the ramp of the 12th Street Bridge.

The bridge was a wreck. She floored it. The old engine groaned in defiance. Cars sat empty and abandoned. Chunks of concrete were missing. Smoke billowed over the river. It wasn't until they were halfway across the bridge that Mason could see the center was completely collapsed.

"Oh, good," he rasped. "Road construction."

A massive gap was opened between the two sides. Mason looked up and then back down at the hole, trying to imagine what could have crashed down to do that much damage.

"What the fuck did that?" He asked because something needed to be said, not because he expected her to know.

"It wasn't a building," Rae said, looking up through the windshield.

It had to be whatever was bringing those alien fucks into the city.

There was no way to drive across. The other side was at least twenty feet away. A jagged shelf of broken rebar and cracked concrete jutted downward toward a lower maintenance platform attached to the bridge's support beam.

Rae brought the Humvee to a stop just a few feet from the edge. For as slow as the thing was, it still screeched and threw Mason forward. He clutched his wrist, panting and howling like the wounded animal he now was.

Rae turned to him, grabbed the shoulder of his hoodie, and tore it off his body with both hands.

"You have to stop getting hurt, man," she said.

"What—why—"

She wrapped his hand in it, cinching it tight with practiced speed.

Mason swallowed back bile. "That's my only—"

"It's a shitty hoodie. For Christ's sake, Mason it's got a fucking swastika on it."

He wheezed as he threw his head backward. He had to remember to breathe. Breathe, not puke, and avoid shitting his pants.

"You're not gonna let that die, are you?"

"I'm not gonna let you die either, so be grateful."

Mason rolled his eyes.

"Don't do me any favors. I'm not sure this is preferable to death at the moment." He held his fucked up hand in the air between them. The hoodie scrap was already sticky with his blood.

Rae rolled her eyes without responding. She turned to the open cargo space in the back of the Humvee. Mason shifted his body to see what was back there as well. If he was lucky, it'd be something he could jam into his eye sockets and end this fucking nightmare.

Instead, they found an M4 carbine with six magazines, a radio kit, and some random gear.

For a moment they just stared. Then, Rae raised her fist.

Mason blinked. "What—"

"Rock, paper, scissors," she said.

"You're shitting me," he replied.

"Best weapon in the apocalypse. We shoot for it."

He stared at her like she'd lost her mind. She playfully wiggled her fingers.

"Ready?"

Reluctantly, he raised his good fist.

"Afghanistan really fucked you up, Rae."

They threw on three.

Mason's hand took the shape of scissors, while Rae threw out a flat hand: paper.

"You've got to be kidding me," she snapped.

Mason grinned through the pain. "Luck of the cripple."

"You bitch," she said.

"Faggot," he shot back.

They both smiled.

He grabbed the M4, slinging it over his shoulder with his good arm. She dropped the magazine in the Beretta. "Five rounds," she said before sliding the magazine back into place.

"You know how to use that, Mason?" Rae asked, eyeing him skeptically.

Outside of his video games, he didn't, but he nodded anyway.

Below the fractured bridge edge, they spotted the narrow metal under-structure—just big enough to crawl onto if they climbed down.

Rae nodded at it. "We go under."

"That is the stupidest plan—"

"You really want to go back?" she challenged. "You saw that big group of them back there."

"Unless you're afraid to swim," she taunted.

"I'm surprised you even know how," he said, meeting her eyes in defiance.

Before she could fire anything back at him, a growl came from behind them: low, familiar, and much too close for comfort. Mason's guts turned to ice.

Rae whipped around, raising her pistol.

The creature was 75 yards away, slowly weaving through the wreckage of cars and bent metal—sniffing at the ground.

Rae sighted the beast in, but with the glitchy way it was moving, Mason didn't see how she could get a good shot.

Its face was shredded like pulled pork. Two of its eyes were torn out. One arm hung loosely. But its jaw still snapped with violent intent. And its gaze locked directly onto the glittering strips of Rae's ruined dress.

Rae fired three rounds, striking the beast at least once on the hind quarters but the creature didn't react. Rae lifted her head and straightened just as the beast leaped in to action.

"That's not good," she said. It was the understatement of a lifetime.

"Oh come on!" Mason shouted upward. "You gave us one minute! One!"

Rae didn't waste time. She grabbed the m4 strap slung across Mason's shoulder like a handle and shoved him toward the broken ledge.

"GO!"

"You're gonna shoot more, right? Right?!"

"You really want me to piss off all his friends?" she asked.

"You have the rifle, mother fucker," she snapped back.

Mason pulled the rifle around to his side and started fumbling with it.

"God dammit, pull the charging handle," she yelled.

He fumbled some more, accidentally ejecting the magazine onto the ground. He looked up at her, heart racing, and realized why she was being so pushy. It wasn't just the shredded beast stalking toward them anymore. An entire group emerged and was now racing in their direction.

"What the fuck, Mason?" The same sharp tone from earlier was in full force. He kept scrambling with the rifle, trying to get the magazine back in place. It was easier in the games he played. In real life, this shit wasn't working.

"Jesus, just go," Rae said. She pushed him toward the ledge.

Mason sat over the broken lip of the mangled bridge. Rae landed next to him, already halfway under the concrete ledge, bare feet dangling over the drop.

The alien screamed, claws scraping asphalt as it launched itself into a frenzy.

Mason dangled his feet over the side, fumbling with his grip. The rifle almost slipped.

Rae reached the maintenance beam and swung under.

"Come on," she ordered.

Mason eyed the cold, dark water below.

As he moved to follow, the alien made contact, tackling him at full force. The impact knocked the air out of his chest. The world spun. He was in mid-air, flying violently. The alien's claws dug into his shirt, shredding through fabric and skin. Its teeth snapped inches from his face.

Chapter 5

The air ripped from his lungs. Mason saw the sky, the water, and Rae's horrified expression above him as she reached down with one hand. Then, the world flipped. They didn't fall clean. The alien slammed into the far end of the broken bridge support. A piece of exposed rebar—jagged, concrete-crusted steel—impaled the creature through the chest.

The momentum jerked them to a stop. Mason swung violently on the alien's weight, the rebar tearing deeper, alien blood spraying as the creature grabbed at the rebar as if it could free itself.

The creature shrieked, claws flailing wildly, one set locked across his stomach, tearing skin and fabric. Mason screamed wordlessly and drove his knife into the top of its forearm. The blade passed all the way through, and Mason gripped the exposed blade with his crudely wrapped hand. He could feel the tearing of flesh as he ripped down toward the creature's wrist, slicing tendon, muscle, and alien sinew. It was like pulling a blade through the center of a stick to split it in two

The creature's grip loosened—but not enough. It had the fight of an alligator.

Above them, Rae braced herself on the maintenance platform. She drew the pistol.

"Don't move," she told him.

"Shoot this fucking thing, Rae!"

She took aim. The alien whipped violently, eyes blazing.

Rae fired once. It was well-targeted into the creature's chest. The second round went into its head.

With the second shot, the creature went still. Its remaining arm loosened.

Finally, it let go, and sent Mason falling 30 feet straight into the cold river below.

The intense cold struck Mason's chest. In his panic to get air, he opened his mouth and water rushed in. He flailed with one arm, the rifle dragging him downward. It was keep the gun or drown. Against all his instincts, he freed himself from the sling and ditched the cumbersome weapon.

Cutting the weight freed him enough to reach the surface for a second before he choked and went under again. The weight was gone, but the water was still so cold that his limbs refused to cooperate. Above him, shapes moved on the bridge. Rae shouted something he couldn't make out. He registered two splashes, the second one much louder than the first. But it wasn't long before the world fell into a muffled silence as he went under again, despite all his flailing.

The rapid thumping in his chest was all he could really feel. This was how it was going to end: a fucking cold plunge? He kicked and swung every part of his body he could move. He just wanted to take a fucking breath. Some part of his brain wanted to live, and that was the part in control in that moment.

His lungs were on fire. His efforts were pointless, but he didn't stop moving. Suddenly, arms wrapped around his chest, dragging his broken, useless body upward. As he reached the surface, a voice coughed in his ear.

"Stop…thrashing…idiot."

He kicked weakly. Each rapid gasp for air left him coughing.

Rae held his head above the surface with one arm. With the other, she pulled them through the water.

"You jumped?!" he wheezed.

"Where's the rifle?" was her reply.

Mason paused. Rae's hands searched the empty space where it should've been.

"It's gone."

"Fuck, Mason."

"I tried to keep a hand on it, but my grip ain't exactly what it used to be," he said, his voice cracking somewhere between panic and offense. He raised the bloody nub out of the water.

The current dragged them downriver in silence as she kept them afloat. Lights from burning buildings reflected off the water in scattered streaks of red and blue. Alien screeches echoed from the bridge behind them.

Rae must have been ambushed after the fall. He wondered if she jumped for him or because she had to.

A large splash came from the water behind them as Rae pulled them toward a marina.

Mason had coughed up half the river and possibly part of his soul as the pair drifted between rows of expensive sailboats. The boats rocked peacefully in the water, completely unfazed by the apocalypse unfolding around them.

"Goddamn, is this how the other side lives?" Mason spat.

Rae snorted. "Yeah. Boats nicer than my house."

"The fucking dock is nicer than mine," he said.

She hauled him toward the nearest yacht—a glossy white monstrosity with chrome rails and a name painted in cursive:

Sea The Day.

Mason gagged as he read it aloud. "I don't know who they are, but I hate them."

"Finally," Rae said. "Something we agree on."

She dragged him up onto the back platform, muscles trembling. He crawled onto the deck and collapsed.

Rae followed, closing the hatch behind them as alien howls faded faintly from far down the river.

Below deck, the cabin smelled like shitty cologne, wine, and old leather. Mason slumped into a leather bench seat, dripping water and blood everywhere. Rae found a towel, tossed it onto his chest, and rummaged through cabinets in the hallway.

"Ah, clothes. I can dry out and not look like an alien snack."

He half-heartedly blotted himself with the towel. Everything was soaked. It seemed pointless. "Little full of ourselves, aren't we?" He raised an eyebrow. "Anything in there I can throw on?"

She held up a black t-shirt with the words, "Bad and Bougie," printed across the front in pink letters.

"Never mind," he said, shaking his head. "I'll stay soggy."

"What?" she said with a laugh. "It's better than, say, Black Lives Matter, don't you think?"

"Don't start," he said. "And I'm not wearing that shirt either." He tilted his head toward the tablecloth-sized shirt she was still holding up.

"You're right," she said too nicely. She dropped the shirt. "Nazi-chic is a much better look."

Before he could respond, she chimed in again.

"In other good news, we do have a first-aid kit. Perfect gift for our broken ex-skinhead!" She tossed it around the closet door to him before ducking behind it to change.

"I'm not a skinhead," he said evenly.

"I said ex-skinhead."

He examined the small assortment of band-aids and ointments. Not even a pain pill in the damn box. "This med kit is trash. Where's the gauze?"

"Rich people don't bleed, apparently," she called from behind the door.

"Ha! They do now." He peered out the small, round window of the vessel.

The landscape outside lit up green as large pods fell to the city below. The glow lit up his face as they appeared and vanished in the distance. She popped out of the closet wearing jeans and a graphic t-shirt. Hers said, *Rich Bitch.*

"Why didn't you offer me that one?" he asked, gesturing toward her chest. "Greedy."

"Shut up," she said, but her voice was playful. She sat down next to him and took his mangled hand with a softness that surprised him.

"Let me see," she said as she examined it.

He winced as she unwrapped the soggy, bloody hoodie scrap. His fingers—well, what was left—looked like someone had tried to erase them all but missed the pinky.

Rae made a face and exhaled. "Yeah. Okay. That's bad." She bit the inside of her cheek while nodding.

"Thanks for the medical opinion, Doctor House."

She returned to the closet door and reemerged with a small bottle of rubbing alcohol.

"Rae," he said. He squeezed both eyes shut before opening them wide. He shook his head, "Nope. Absolutely no—"

She poured it over the wound.

Mason's scream reverberated through the small space.

"Should've warned you," she said casually. "My bad."

"Fuck! You're a psychopath. A goddamn psychopa—"

"Hold still," she growled.

She bandaged it as best she could. It wasn't pretty. But it was cleaner, and the bleeding slowed.

When she finished, she moved to his leg and examined it.

She leaned back and sighed

"Fuck, okay," she said. "Give me a minute with this one.

For a long moment, neither of them spoke as she cut away the torn denim from the wound.

Then Mason said, low and steady, as if stating a fact rather than a confession.

"I was going to kill myself tonight."

Rae didn't turn. She didn't rush to answer. She just kept gently peeling the bloody fabric from his leg. Her eyes were locked on the task in front of her, but she bit at the inside of her cheek.

After a moment, she said, "That decision doesn't expire. You can make it later."

He looked at her with an unsettled grin. Her bluntness surprised him.

Her voice remained even. "Is that why you came outside guns blazing? You decided you didn't want to die as a quitter?"

A short, bitter breath escaped him. "I quit a long time ago," he said. "I've lived my whole life afraid to stand up and bailing when the choices got hard. That makes me a coward."

Rae kept studying his leg. He knew the wound was deep, but he didn't think that was why her eyes stayed on it.

"Fear governs everyone," she said. "The difference isn't whether it exists. It's whether you obey it."

Mason considered her words.

"When you came out of that building," she continued, "you were afraid. I could see it. But you moved anyway."

She turned to him then.

"I didn't see a weak man. I saw a man who accepted that his death was inevitable. Someone who made a hard choice. I saw someone who acted while scared shitless. That's courage."

Mason swallowed.

"Fear can reduce grown men to children," Rae said, "or it can harden a person into something capable."

She held his gaze.

"You don't ever eliminate fear. You discipline it."

They looked at each other, and Mason smiled at Rae.

"When did find out"? He asked after a second or two.

Her brow furrowed. "To discipline my fear?" she asked.

He shook his head. "No, when did you find out you were so gay?" Mason clenched through his smile, bracing for a punch.

Instead, Rae gave his leg a squeeze.

"Okay, okay, stop," he begged.

She shook her head with a smile. Her eyes fell back to Mason's gory leg. Blood was seeping through the bandage Rae had already peeled back twice. She tilted her head from side to side while she stared. He wasn't sure what she was considering, but he was sure he wasn't going to like it.

After a few more head tilts, she lifted a Bic lighter to his line of sight. Where the fuck had she gotten that from?

"No," he said calmly. He shook his head as hard as he could. "That's where this ends, you crazy bitch."

Rae held the lighter a few inches from his thigh. "You're still bleeding and we don't have enough gauze to pack the wound."

"Yeah, well," Mason muttered, "You're still not a doctor.

And you're black. And a woman," he shook his head in fake disappointment. "That's three strikes, Rae. I don't make the rules…"

She glanced up at him, eyes full of annoyance.

"See? We can all say crazy things." His voice cracked. If he couldn't reason with her, he could try to distract her from this awful idea with humor…or anger. Whatever worked.

"Look Mason, either I burn it, or I stuff it shut… or you bleed out."

"What's behind door number four?" Mason asked.

Rae still didn't look impressed. "You're afraid of pain. I get it. Don't be a pussy."

"I'm afraid of everything," Mason said. "Pain's just very fucking persuasive."

She sparked the lighter once. "Terrible response," she said. "I might have been persuaded by a joke about how you are what you eat. But that answer simply won't do."

She moved the lighter closer to his leg.

Mason flinched and squeezed his eyes shut. He wasn't going to win this one.

"Can I at least have some rum? I can't do this shit sober."

Before she could answer, the cabin creaked. Her head snapped up. She released the lighter.

Not the usual boat noises. The air was static and thick. Glass trinkets hanging from the ceiling began to sway. A low vibration rolled through the hull, like something big clearing its throat. The sound got deeper—fast.

Pressure crawled up Mason's spine.

Rae straightened. "Brace," she said.

"Wha—" Mason began, but there wasn't time for him to finish his question. The rear of the yacht caved inward. Wood tore.

Metal screamed. Mason was thrown sideways. Trinkets and supplies rocked and were thrown from the cabinets.

"That was not how you warn someone to brace themselves, Rae," he shouted.

Water flooded in from the stern of the vessel as the boat regained control and the waves settled.

Rae stood and looked at Mason, her stance low and her brow furrowed. "What the fuck was that?" she asked.

She staggered toward the back of the boat, Mason on her tail. They stepped through — and in Mason's case, tripped over— piles of debris. Beyond the torn hull, the river was black—but something glowed beneath it.

Mason craned his neck, trying to make out what it was. A green orb glowed beneath the murky water. It pierced the ship and embedded itself into the muddy riverbed below.

Mason squinted. "Is that… alien luggage?"

"It must be some kind of drop pod, maybe?" Rae said. "Reinforcements?" He didn't know why she bothered making it sound like a question. She rarely seemed to question herself, even when talking about literal fucking aliens.

"Good," Mason muttered. "I was worried they were all done."

The yacht groaned again.

"We're leaving," Rae said. "Now."

"You think those things can swim?" Mason asked, peeking over the side of the vessel.

Rae grabbed his shoulder and turned him toward the dock. "Doesn't matter." She gave his back a small shove. "Because we're getting the fuck out of here."

She was wrong. It did matter. Because that's when the water erupted.

A creature surged up, claws ripping into the shattered stern.

It latched onto the wreckage, trying to haul itself out. River water poured from its open mouth.

Mason screamed. "Fuck. They can swim. Fuck!"

Rae shoved him backward. "Move."

She grabbed a decorative wooden oar from behind him and swung.

CRACK.

The oar smashed into the creature's skull as it tried to climb aboard, stopping its progress.

Mason scrambled away on his back, dragging himself toward the cabin. "Kill that fish-alien-fuck, Rae!"

Rae hit it again.

And again. "What's it look like I'm trying to do, Mason?"

The creature gurgled, blood and river water bubbling from its lungs. One eye socket collapsed inward. Something wet sprayed across Rae's face as she hit it again.

Mason froze. "Rae… you've got fucking brains on you."

"Tracking," she said, swinging again. This time, she added more time between the strikes, but each blow landed with a louder crack.

She didn't stop until the skull collapsed completely. The creature went limp—but its claws were buried deep in the wood, locking it to the ass end of the boat.

Rae just stood there, chest rising high with each breath. Gore was splattered across her new shirt and jeans—it even peppered her face.

Mason stared. "Holy… fucking… shit… Rae!"

She put the splintered ore against the alien's chest and pushed. The claws finally slipped free. The body slid back into the river, skull fragments breaking away. Pale bits of brain floated to the surface with the air bubbles. It looked like some kind of fucked-up witch's brew.

Mason gagged. "That's fucking disgusting." The smell was too much. The visual wasn't helping. He held back the first gag, but he couldn't stop the second one. He lurched forward and puked all over the deck.

"Keep it together, man. Shit," she said as she wiped her face with the back of her hand. On the second swipe, she smeared the brain fragments straight across her mouth.

She froze. Her hand was still inches from her face. She stared at it. Her chin quivered.

"Oh fuck," was all she managed before gagging once and doubling over to puke right next to him.

Mason wiped his mouth and spat. "Keep it together, Rae. Shit," he mocked.

"Fuck off," she rasped. She coughed and spat a few more times before she straightened. She scrubbed her hands against her jeans.

The yacht creaked again as water climbed higher. Below them, the green glow pulsed and then went dark.

Mason glanced at it and sighed. "I was just playing God; we can slow down the full-send apocalypse now."

Rae wiped her mouth, eyes hard. "Get up."

He just looked at her.

"We have to move. The boat is sinking," she said.

The boat tilted as the ropes that tied it to the dock popped under the pressure.

Mason's heart raced, but all he managed to do was blink at her.

"We need a plan," she said, locking eyes with him. "My brother's place is across town. We can still get there."

Mason took a breath. "Okay, well I hate to point out the

obvious here, but your plans keep getting me fucked up."

He held up his nub of a hand, waving it at her. It was a painful way to get the point across, but worth it.

"You're alive, aren't you?" Her voice was calm. So goddamn calm.

"True, but we have one knife and no car. What's the plan? How do we fight these things?"

Rae scanned the wreckage at her feet. "We have tools," she said, holding up a boat oar and a rusted wrench she pulled from the debris. "Improvisation is the soul of survival."

He sighed. "You're insane."

"Again, let me point out that you're still alive."

"Am I supposed to be thanking you for that?"

"No," she said. "You're supposed to shut the fuck up and get off the damn boat, Mason."

"You're supposed to shut the fuck up, Mason," he mimicked under his breath. "Get off the damn boat, Mason."

"What was that?" she asked.

"Nothing," he said quickly. "I'm getting off the damn boat."

They grabbed some stale crackers, bottled water, and rum before climbing off the sinking boat. The two of them sat in exhausted silence until early dawn, watching the boat sink from the dock and re-wrapping Mason's leg with the little gauze they had left. Neither of them slept. They just sat and watched—listened for every possible threat, and hoped each strange sound wouldn't bring a fresh new hell their way.

Their luck held. After several hours, the morning sun repainted the dark, smoky sky a deep purple-red. They stood together without a word, and Mason followed Rae onto the river path. They began the trip to Rae's brother's house.

Chapter 6

Mason limped. Rae led.

The river glowed orange from the pending sunrise and distant fires.

After an hour of silence, Rae froze and raised her fist.

Mason's steps halted.

Ahead, flames flickered against a brick wall. Shadows—tall, twisted, hunched—moved in jerky patterns. Not human.

Rae leaned close and whispered, "We can't go through there."

Mason tightened his grip on his knife.

"So what? Backtrack?"

She pointed toward the narrow spillway running perpendicular to the riverbank—dark, wet, narrow, and echoing.

"That's our way through."

Mason swallowed.

"That's a death trap."

"Everything's a death trap," she said. "Pick yours."

He stared at her. Then at the inlet. Then at the burning city. He sighed.

"Fine," he said. "But if we die, I'm blaming God."

Rae smirked. "That's all you do."

They silently slipped down to the inlet entrance and into the darkness.

They weren't in the tunnels long before Mason's bandage was damp with sweat, blood, and the slow creep of whatever moisture lived down here permanently. He didn't want to fucking look at it. It made him sick. If he stared too closely, his brain might process how bad this shit actually was, and he didn't have the energy or the strength in his stomach for that kind of argument with himself.

His leg throbbed beneath its wrappings, heat trapped tight under layers of dirty cloth. Every step sent a sharp pulse up into his hip, like his thigh was trying to warn him about something he already knew. There was no way this wasn't infected. Instinctively, he thought about the bills this would lead to, but the world ending helped him grapple with his mountainous piles of debt.

He kept looking up at Rae and past her into the dark passageways—the shallow black water ahead of them swallowed light instead of reflecting it.

He studied her as her bare feet trudged the path ahead of him. Could she really get them out of this mess? Why exactly was he putting his life in her hands? Maybe just because it didn't matter anymore. Or maybe it did. He wasn't sure.

She glided through the narrow passageways of the tunnels like they had been built with her in mind.

She stayed low, shoulders angled forward, chin tucked just enough to protect her neck. Her eyes never stopped scanning— hidden corners and overhead seams. She hugged every wall like a gunman was waiting on the other side—her movements were swift and intentional, and every part of her body seemed to know exactly what it was doing.

She carried the splintered boat oar in both hands like a spear, the wood dark with old blood that flaked off in dry curls when she shifted her grip. A rusted wrench rode her waistband, heavy and ugly, looking like it deployed with her overseas.

Mason had a knife and a shitty attitude; that was the only thing keeping him upright.

"Tell me again how this isn't retarded as fuck," he whispered.

His voice sounded off down here—flattened, chewed up by concrete, bounced back at him a half second late like someone else was repeating it just out of sight.

Rae didn't look back. "Because the alternative is dying in the light."

"Yeah," he started, "dying in piss and darkness is a clear winner." His breath fogged faintly in the damp air.

"Stop bitching, Mason. Your voice travels," she snapped.

The tunnel split ahead of them—concrete arteries branching left and right, both equally narrow, both equally confusing. Old stencils clung to the walls, arrows and numbers half-eaten by rust and mold; old graffiti stained everything. Standing water pooled ankle-deep, opaque and greasy, rippling faintly as something moved far away.

Neither of them had slept for forty-eight hours. The exhaustion sat on them like stacked bricks on a collapsing foundation. Every sound felt louder than it should have been. Every decision felt heavier. Stress layered on stress until Mason felt like he was holding himself together with friction alone.

The air was thick. Not just sewage—though that was definitely there—but mold, iron, stagnant water, and a sour rot that had soaked into the concrete over decades. It tasted like pennies and mildew and something vaguely chemical. Every breath felt like borrowing time from a body that was already overdrawn.

Mason stared down the left passage, then the right.

"These all look like mouths," he said.

"They're paths," Rae replied.

"Yeah," he muttered. "Funny how I keep letting you pick which one eats us."

Her shoulders dipped—just barely. He almost missed it. Then she straightened.

"Then where, Mason?" she asked quietly. "Speak now or forever fucking hold your tongue."

The challenge wasn't loud. That made it worse.

He scoffed, sharp and defensive. "Do you ever hear yourself?"

Her eyes flicked to his hand: the bandage, his hanging arm. She didn't say anything. She didn't have to.

"You follow," she said, "but you bitch the whole way. Every plan's stupid. Every move's wrong. And when it doesn't go exactly how you imagined—"

"I don't imagine shit," he snapped. "I react. That's called being smart."

She laughed once. Not mocking. Just tired.

"No," Rae said. "That's called indecisiveness."

Something in his chest tightened.

"There it is," he said. "That look. Like I'm the dumbest guy in the room again."

"That's not what I said."

"It's what everyone means," he shot back. "Teachers. Guards. Cops. You. Like I'm one bad thought away from fucking it all up."

Her jaw set.

"You do fuck it up," she said.

He flinched, then leaned into it. "Because I follow you. Because you always know what to do. You're always decisive. Always right. But nobody believes in me. Shit, nobody even gives me a shot. But you…you have the *gift.* I gave you a shot, and now look at me." His voice rose despite himself. "I'm the idiot limping behind you, paying for it."

She stared at him—really stared.

"You think I don't get hurt?" she asked quietly.

"I think you don't bleed," Mason said. He gestured at himself. "You make the call, I get hurt, and then you look at me like I failed a test I didn't know we were taking."

"That's not fair. I gave you a shot, Mason. It's a two-way street."

"No, it's not," he snapped. "But funny how you never question yourself when things go bad. It's always just—keep moving. Keep pushing. Leave whoever can't keep up."

Her eyes sharpened.

"Careful," she warned.

He swallowed. Then said it anyway.

"Worked out great for your friend."

The words landed heavier than he expected.

Rae went still. Not frozen—contained. Like something dangerous had just been locked behind glass.

"You don't get to say that," she said.

"You left," he shot back. "You said it yourself. Too loud. Too much. You walked out, and the world ended."

Her breathing changed. Slower. Measured.

"You don't know a fucking thing about that night," she said.

"Maybe not," Mason said. "But I know what it's like to be the one who gets left. To watch someone decide you're… expendable."

"That's not what happened."

"That's always what happens," he said. "People with options move on. People like me just get in the way."

"Cut the pity party bullshit, Mason. It's not that you're in the way because you're trying to help. You're in the way because you're too busy tearing everything down." Rae said finally, voice tight. "Every plan. Every decision. And when it's time to choose—you freeze. Then you get mad at the fallout."

"Maybe because every time I choose, it ends the same."

"You don't choose," she said. "You wait for it to fail so you can say you knew it would."

"You think I like quitting?" he said, low and raw. "You think I wake up wanting to feel useless?"

Her eyes softened. That hurt worse than anger.

"I think," she said, "you'd rather hate yourself than risk finding out you might be wrong."

He swallowed hard.

"You don't walk away," she continued. "You get carried. And then you resent the people doing the carrying."

"I never asked you to."

"I know," Rae said. "That's the tragedy."

They stood there—her steady, him shaking—fear humming between them like exposed wire.

"You want to lead so bad," she said, "then tell me where we're going."

Mason kicked at the water with his good foot, refusing to answer.

She looked at him.

"And you wonder why I don't put my life in your hands," she said. "You won't decide. And when you do, you don't follow through." Her voice dropped. "We only met because you tried to kill yourself and backed out."

Heat surged up his throat.

"Fuck you," he said, barely audible. "You've got some fucking nerve."

"Your reactions get people hurt," Rae said. "And what scares me is you don't even seem to care."

He barked a laugh. "I don't care? I saved *your* ass."

"You saved *your* ass," she shot back. "I just happened to benefit."

"Guess that makes me your lucky charm," he said. "Bodies pile up, I walk away, and you pretend that bothers you."

She braced, ready to answer—he knew whatever she said next was going to piss him off even more, but she never got the chance. Metal popped somewhere behind them.

Rae's head snapped toward the sound instantly, body coiling.

"We'll finish this later," she whispered. She turned and took the left corridor. Mason followed for now.

Above ground, the city's chaos sounded the same. Down below, there was only dripping water, the soft slap of movement in the dark, and their breathing echoing back at them like someone else was following just out of sight.

Rae's bare feet made quiet, sticky sounds against the concrete: skin against slime. Each step left a faint wet print that vanished as water seeped back over it. Mason couldn't stop noticing. Couldn't stop thinking about what coated the floor—sewage residue, rust flakes, old chemical runoff, biological leftovers that had soaked into the concrete long before last night ever happened.

The walls glistened, coated in a thin film that reflected light eerily. Moisture traced slow paths downward, dripping from seams overhead and plinking into the water around their ankles. Somewhere above them, something scuttled inside the walls.

Mason's boots splashed with every step: loud and clumsy. He

hated the noise. Hated how it felt like announcing himself to everything that might be listening.

The tunnel narrowed. The ceiling dropped. He hunched forward, leg screaming.

Something skittered ahead—fast, low, too many feet.

"Still think I'm the dangerous one?" he whispered.

Rae didn't answer. That silence felt like agreement.

The corridor fed into a maintenance maze—intersecting spillways, half-flooded walkways, rusted ladders bolted into walls that led to sealed hatches or collapsed ceilings. Some paths looped back on themselves. Others ended in grated dead ends choked with debris and bones that might or might not have been animal.

Standing water swallowed their ankles, cold and thick, sucking at Mason's boots when he lifted his feet. The smell intensified, crawling into his sinuses and refusing to leave.

They marked their turns without speaking—chalk lines scratched into concrete, bits of fabric torn and tied to ladder rungs, blood smears Mason didn't remember making. The maze didn't want them to leave. It folded back on itself, identical corridors repeating until Mason started to feel like he was walking inside a thought that he couldn't resolve.

You're not only selfish, you're fucking reckless.

Rae's words replayed in his head like a bad recording. He wasn't trying to be selfish. Or to hurt anyone. That was never the fucking point. He was just trying to get by: to survive. He didn't just go around dragging other people into his shit. But still, she wasn't wrong. And that truth burned inside him like its own kind of infection.

Suddenly, a shape appeared ahead. Mason raised his knife, heart spiking—then hesitated. This movement was different.

Not predatory. Not hunting.

A flicker of light danced across the walls.

"Rae," he whispered. "I think it's a person."

A woman sat slumped against the wall, knees pulled tight to her chest. A flashlight trembled in her hand, its beam spasming on and off like it might die any second. She wore a backpack that bulged at odd angles, straps cutting into her shoulders. Her shoes were soaked. Her face was gray with shock.

Rae crouched slowly. "Hey. It's okay."

The woman flinched hard. "Don't come closer."

Her eyes locked onto Rae's shirt—dark stains, bits of something dried and clinging stubbornly. Then onto Mason's knife and his torn hoodie.

"You're... together?" she whispered.

"We're moving through," Rae said. "You alone?"

The woman swallowed. "My husband—" Her voice cracked. "We hid. Then it got quiet and—"

She folded inward, forehead pressed to her knees, shoulders shaking.

Mason watched her and felt irritation before sympathy. Not at the grief—but at the posture. The waiting. The hope that someone else would decide what happened next.

He'd worn that shape once. In a cell. Before he learned to harden it into something safer.

"What's in the bag?" he asked.

The woman stiffened.

Rae shot him a look. "Mason."

"We need supplies," he said.

"We're not robbing people."

"She's sitting dry with a light and gear while you're barefoot and I'm bleeding," he snapped. "That's not theft. That's math."

Rae stepped closer to him. "Listen to yourself."

The woman scrambled back along the wall, panic climbing fast. "Please—"

Rae turned, anger slipping through her control. "Back off."

Mason laughed once. "You wanted me to make a decision, right? Well, I'm making one. We take what we need and we keep moving."

Rae's voice went flat. "I will kill you if you force this."

That did it. Mason saw it then—clear as day. Not hatred. Duty.

He spat into the water. "That's fine. You stay here with the corpse bride. She's too frozen to argue with you. I'm sure that's gonna work out nicely." He turned and limped away, boots splashing loudly.

"Don't be a bitch," Rae called.

"Don't be a fucking saint," he shot back.

He walked back into the maze of tunnels

"Mason," Rae hissed, "Mason!" He walked away, not looking back, and disappeared into the darkness.

He walked aimlessly for what felt like hours. He stopped at another corridor. Hadn't he just seen that one? He looked in both directions, then down at his feet. Everything looked the fucking same. Had Rae even known she was taking them somewhere, or had she just been wandering like he was now?

He looked down at the mess of his hand and tried to decide which way to move. Finally, he dropped to his knees in the muck.

"Fuck, why am I like this?" he yelled to no one. He let out a sound that was more animal than man—all desperation and pain.

He stayed there for a minute and pondered how his life went south so fast after high school. The conversation with Rae left him spun out; the fatigue was weighing on him. He couldn't find her if he wanted to; he was already lost, and it had only been 30, maybe 45 minutes. Mason respected her but hated that she was easily a better person than him. She could care and be stern and driven in all the ways he struggled.

"You really fucked this one up, Mason," he said.

Then, a voice from behind him echoed, "You did fuck up, boy."

A figure grabbed him fast. A hand clamped over his mouth. Fingers dug into his jaw hard enough to bruise. Another body slammed him into the wall, knocking the air from his lungs.

His knife clattered away, skidding into the water.

"Quiet," a voice hissed in his ear, deep and rumbling. The breath smelled like sweat, cigarettes, and metal.

Another set of hands grabbed his arms, wrenching his bad hand. Pain exploded, and he bit down on the palm over his mouth until he tasted blood.

Mason fought—knee, elbow, teeth—wild and clumsy with exhaustion and injury.

"Jesus, he's feral," someone said.

They dragged him sideways into a narrow side passage, boots splashing, bodies bumping into rusted pipes. The corridor swallowed them, light vanishing behind a bend, the maze closing like a throat.

For the first time since the gun-in-mouth moment, Mason felt real fear.

It was a fear he remembered all too well—not of dying, but of being powerless.

Chapter 7

They didn't take him far. Just far enough.

A utility room with an old pump station, rusted control panels, plastic chairs, and a workbench with tools long-stolen. It looked as though they had made it into a makeshift home before the apocalypse landed. A dim red safety light buzzed overhead sporadically.

Two men—battered and exhausted-looking. Both were armed, but not with guns. They held blades and pipes and the kind of desperate eyes that he'd seen in prisoners who should have been in psych wards.

One of them had a bandage on his forearm soaked through with blood.

The other had a broken nose that still looked fresh.

They shoved Mason into a chair.

He tried to stand. His leg buckled. The pain had traversed into something deeper—the way festering wounds tend to do.

"Sit," one of them growled.

Mason stared at them, breathing hard through his nose.

"Who the fuck are you?" he rasped.

The guy with the broken nose leaned in. "Who the fuck are you?"

Mason's eyes scanned the room for exits, but only found one.

Trash littered the floor around them like they'd been there for a while. Even if he got away, would they know this place well enough to find him? Especially in his fucked-up state.

"Apparently tonight's theme is retarded introductions," he said.

Mason tensed, ready to charge.

Broken Nose Guy shoved a pipe to Mason's throat. "Try it."

Mason held still. His eyes flicked to the pipe, then up.

"You guys want something, or are we fucking?" he said.

Bandage Guy opened Mason's wrapped hand with a grimace, staring at the missing fingers like he was looking at a price tag.

"You got hurt fighting those things," bandage guy said. "That means you got something."

Mason's jaw clenched. "Yeah. Fucking trauma."

Bandage guy ignored the sarcasm. "jewelry. Ammo. Food. Something shiny. They like shiny things."

Mason stared at him. "If I had ammo, you think I'd be sitting here with a pipe to my neck? No, I'd be up there robbing banks and telling God and everyone to fuck off."

Broken-nose guy smirked. "He's funny."

Bandage guy didn't smile. "He's a fucking smart ass."

"I wonder how many funny jokes he'll tell after this," Bandage guy reached down and gripped Mason's crotch.

Mason swallowed. What the fuck had he just fallen into? All the years in prison, dodging this exact fate, only to be raped in a tunnel during an alien invasion. Why did the world want him to go out like a bitch so badly?

Rae's words echoed: You don't ever eliminate fear. You discipline it.

He hated that she was right.

And he hated more that he'd walked away.

Because now he was alone. Just like he was in the pen, alone like he'd been with his old gang leader, Bailey. Bailey would have fit right in with these two. They all had the same crazed look in their eyes. He felt as sick and anxious now as he had back then.

Mason's eyes shifted—he listened.

From somewhere far off in the tunnel, he heard her voice. Rae?

Rae was calling his name.

It hit his chest like a punch.

She'd followed.

Of course she did. Because Rae couldn't fucking help herself. Because she did the hard thing even when it pissed her off.

Mason's throat tightened.

He forced a lazy grin. "Your plan kinda sucks, you know that?"

Bandage guy snarled. "Shut the fuck up."

Mason kept his voice loud, teasing—bait. "You two are doing great, though. Real professional kidnapping. Love the ambiance. Smells like piss and failure. You two faggots get a lot of cocks down here or what?"

Broken-nose guy raised the pipe like he was going to swing.

Mason leaned into it, eyes wide. "Do it," he shouted. He launched spit right at Bandage Guy's face.

The men hesitated. And that half-second was enough.

Rae came out of the dark like a ghost with anger issues.

She didn't shout. She didn't warn. She drove the boat oar straight into the Broken-nose Guy's throat.

He wheezed, grabbing his neck, collapsing.

Bandage Guy spun, knife up.

Rae slammed the wrench into his wrist. The knife clattered

to the floor. She kicked it away and drove her elbow into his throat, hard enough to make him gag and fold.

Mason surged up out of the chair, adrenaline flooding. With his good hand he grabbed the fallen pipe and brought it down as hard as he could across Bandage Guy's temple.

The man dropped, eyes bulged out of the sockets, ears pouring some kind of clear liquid.

Rae kicked the other man into the ankle deep water and mounted him one hand clamped on his throat holding his face just below water and drove her other fist into his face repeatedly until his gurgled breathes filled his lungs with water and he shook violently then stopped moving

Silence snapped back in.

Rae stood over the lifeless body, her chest rising and falling, her eyes furious.

Mason stared at her. In that moment, she reminded him of the posters back in his apartment. He didn't know what to say.

Then he said the dumbest honest thing in his head.

"You followed me."

Rae wiped her mouth with the back of her hand. "Yeah, I'm a real idiot sometimes."

"Where's the girl?" he asked.

"She couldn't move. Frozen in fear. You were right."

He looked at his shaking hands for a moment yea "Yeah, fear," he said under his breath

Mason's voice went quiet. "Why did you come back for me?"

Rae's glare sharpened. "Don't make this gay mason."

Mason swallowed. "I'm not trying to—"

Rae stepped closer until she was in his space, and her voice dropped to a hard whisper.

"You don't get to walk away and die just because you're angry," she said. "Not if you're going to keep dragging other people into your orbit."

Mason flinched at the truth of it. Even though it felt more like she had brought him into hers.

Rae's jaw clenched. "You want to be reckless? Fine. Be reckless with your life. But stop making me clean up after you."

Mason's throat worked. He looked away.

"I didn't ask you to follow," he muttered.

Rae's eyes went colder. "No. You just walked off like a child because I told you the truth."

Mason's anger flashed—automatic.

Then died.

Because he saw it—just for a moment—behind her rage: fear.

Not of monsters.

Of losing control. Of losing someone. Of failing again.

Mason exhaled slowly.

"I don't know how to do this," he said, voice low. "The… team shit. The trust shit."

Rae stared at him like she was deciding whether to punch him.

Mason kept going anyway.

"In prison, you pick a side or you get eaten," he said. "So I picked. And I did what I had to do. And now you keep looking at me like I'm that guy forever."

Rae didn't soften. But she didn't look away either.

Mason swallowed hard. "And maybe I am. Maybe that's all I am."

Rae's voice dropped. "No."

One word. Flat. Certain.

Mason blinked.

Rae pointed at his hand. "That guy would've used me as bait and run." She pointed at the dead men. "That guy would've joined them." Then she jabbed a finger into Mason's chest. "You didn't."

Mason's breath caught.

Rae stepped back, pulling herself together like she always did. "Let's go," she said. "Before any more come. Before anything else hears us."

Mason bent and picked up his knife from the water, tucking it into his waistband. He hesitated, then grabbed the smaller of the two pipes and handed it to Rae.

She stared at it, then took it without comment.

He kicked at the boots of one of the bodies, looking at Rae.

"What do you think those are? About a size 10?"

"It doesn't matter," she said, bending down to pull them off the dead guy's feet. "I've already got hepatitis from walking in this shit barefoot. Who cares if they fit."

"Does this count as robbery?" he said with a smile as she laced them up and stood.

"Shut the fuck up," was her only reply.

They moved back into the tunnel.

As they walked, Mason kept a half-step behind her, quieter now. Watching her shoulders. Watching how she held the pipe like it was temporary, like she still expected to find a better weapon.

After a long stretch of silence, Mason finally said, "I'm sorry."

Rae didn't look back. "Don't do it again."

Mason huffed a laugh. "That's not forgiveness."

Rae's voice was dry. she turned to him

"When did you figure it out, Mason?"

"Figure what out," Mason said nervously.

"When did you figure out you're a faggot?" She said with a grin.

Mason smiled and shook his head. "I mean it, though. I really am sorry. I hate feeling like a burden, and right now I'm literally dead weight."

"You save me. I save you. We rinse. We repeat. That's how this team shit works, okay? It's that simple, and it's that hard."

Mason nodded. "Okay, deal," he said. She gave a small nod and turned. They followed the tunnel's bend until the air shifted—less wet, more smoke. Light began to bloom ahead, pale and gray.

Dawn was breaking.

The tunnel mouth opened upward through a broken utility hatch.

Rae went first, peeking out and listening.

Then she climbed.

Mason followed, muscles shaking, leg screaming, hand throbbing in time with his pulse.

They emerged into daylight.

And the world above looked like it had survived the night by accident.

They climbed out into a strip mall parking lot.

Around them, the scene was full of smoke from burned trash cans. Cars lay abandoned. Evidence from the night's chaos was everywhere. The sun's light brought the reality of this mess into plain view.

Rae exhaled once, slow. Mason studied her profile—the determined set of her jaw was back. The certainty in her stance was unmistakable.

For the first time since the yacht, they stood side by side

without feeling like they might kill each other. They weren't friends—at least not yet. But they were together. And that was enough to keep them both going.

Chapter 8

The two of them took in the surrounding scene. Behind the parking lot full of smoke and cars, a boarded-up liquor store leaned as if it was too tired to keep standing. Mason caught movement from the far end of the parking lot.

As they approached the strip mall, Mason saw a black man in his early thirties stumble out from between two burned-out storefronts. His hoodie was torn down one sleeve; cargo pants soaked at the knees. He waved once, then stopped short, staring at them as if he wasn't sure they were real.

"Hey—hey—" the man said. His voice wobbled. "You can see me, right?"

Behind him, a boy—no more than eight—clung to his leg, fingers knotted in fabric, eyes wide and glassy. He didn't make a sound.

"They came through the windows," the man said suddenly, like he was correcting himself. "Just—through them. Like the glass wasn't even there."

He dragged a hand over his face, breathing too fast.

"My wife had the baby," he went on. "She was holding him. I told her to get down. I told her—"

His voice broke.

"They pulled them out," he whispered. "I couldn't—I couldn't—"

The words collapsed into a sound that wasn't language.

Rae didn't hesitate. She moved toward him immediately.

Mason followed, limping, vision blurring. The man kept talking, repeating pieces of the same sentence like they might rearrange themselves into something survivable.

Mason recognized the look. He'd seen it before—panic stripped of logic, guilt clawing for a shape it could live in.

The man collapsed to his knees, gripping Rae's hands. "I lost her—I lost them. The monsters came. I tried, I tried—my boy—the baby, his toy car, he saw everything."

His sobs cracked like gunshots in the quiet morning. The boy's eyes darted from Rae to Mason. There was no light there—just emptiness. It was the worst kind of nothing—because you could tell there used to be so much more in its place.

Rae knelt, pulling the boy close. Her voice dropped, low and lethal—the kind of soft that promised blood.

"You're safe now. Both of you." It was a lie, Mason knew, but maybe a necessary one.

Mason swallowed hard. The air was thick with a hopeless grief—the kind that carves you out from the inside. Mason knew it too well.

"My name is Rae," she said. "This is Mason. We're heading somewhere safe. We can help you. Come with us."

The man nodded, tears choking him as he mumbled to himself.

Mason knew exactly why Rae took the two of them in. The man had obviously lost his mind. If they left the boy with his father alone, it would be a day—maybe two at most—before they'd be dead.

And just like that, the man and his son were part of their group. Rae said the word, and just like Mason, the two of them joined the ranks. No questions or hesitations. They just believed her.

Rae was the calm in the storm: the anchor. He was used to the way people looked at him when they met him. Suspicion and wariness always played across their faces. He had no idea what it felt like to be the kind of person people met and instantly trusted—instantly wanted to follow. He didn't know how she did it. He only knew she could.

The daylight brought heat and haze. The monsters stayed back, sluggish in the sun, their heads twitching like broken metronomes. A cursed truce, Mason thought. They watched. Waited. But didn't come.

Mason thought the sun shining on everything would make the creatures more active. More vicious. But none of them were attacking anything—it was like they were too exhausted.

"Why aren't they coming after us?" he finally asked out loud.

Rae stopped and scanned. She tilted her head slightly. "I don't know. It can't be the light." She wiped at her brow. "Maybe the heat?"

Whatever it was, he was thankful for the pause in the action. It would be nice to have some time to catch their breath.

But the break didn't last long. Rae led them behind the strip mall, toward the wooded edge near the overpass: safer ground.

It was then that Mason heard the whistle. Not a whistle. The whistle.

Short. Sharp. Familiar. Bile rose in his throat.

"Shit," he whispered, stopping mid-step. The fucking apocalypse was bad enough. He was fighting aliens, for fuck's sake. This—this was too much.

Rae turned. "What is it?"

Mason's voice came out flat. "This is bad, Rae. We need to get the fuck out of here."

But it was too late. Three men stepped into view from behind a concrete pillar. They were white men covered in ink. They all wore the same combat boots. Mason would have known them even without knowing them. They were hate in human form: the Aryan Brotherhood.

And at the head of the pack stood Bailey. Bailey, the ringleader of every mistake Mason made back in prison.

Mason looked at the sky. "You motherfucker," he mouthed. God had no problem letting Mason swallow lead, but he hadn't found time to kill this piece of shit off yet? Maybe cockroaches really could survive the apocalypse.

"Well, wait just a minute!"

Mason flinched at the sound of Bailey's voice.

Bailey stepped into view, holding a machete in one hand. The blade, which someone had wiped but not cleaned, was nicked and darkened with old gore. A pistol sat tucked into his waistband, angled just right, like it was on display.

His gray zip-front hoodie was filthy at the cuffs and collar, sweat-soaked and stiff with days of wear. Black denim jeans hung low on his hips, torn at the knees and thighs, smeared with grime and something that had dried too dark to question.

But his face was clean.

Shaved close. Jawline sharp. Not a cut or smear on his skin. He'd taken the time. Probably admired the result in a cracked mirror somewhere while the world burned.

His eyes were bright and confident, scanning Mason like an appraisal. He stood loose and comfortable, the posture of someone who'd already figured out how to enjoy this new version of things.

Bailey smiled—wide, satisfied, proud of himself. That smile showed up in too many of Mason's worst memories. And almost all of his worst nightmares.

"Bailey—" Mason started, but was cut short before he could continue.

"Don't!" Bailey's voice filled the air, loud and booming, before breaking into a strange, monotone laugh. His broad shoulders shook as the laughs came out in short, psychotic bursts.

"No, Mason," Bailey said. His eyes were wide and wild. He scratched his head with the machete.

"We don't see each other, do we, Mason?"

Mason knew nature of any conversation with Bailey. He'd learned the hard way. He hoped Rae and the others would just keep their mouths shut.

"Of course we don't, Bailey," he said. He was mustering every ounce of calm he had inside him.

"Don't!" Bailey shouted again. This time, the word cut in and out as he screamed.

Before anyone could process his rage, Bailey's posture changed along with his tone. His shoulders relaxed. He smiled with a tilt of his head.

"Don't talk when I'm talking," he said with a calm that was more unnerving than his screams.

None of Mason's group moved. They all stood, eyes glued to the chaos, as Bailey paced back and forth in front of them. After a few seconds of pacing, he knelt down to grab a handful of loose dirt.

"We don't see each other," he said as he stood. "That was the rule. Do you remember, Mason?"

Bailey shook his hands full of dirt like dice; dust cascaded from his fingers. "Hmm?"

Mason swallowed again, but said nothing.

Bailey swung the blade lazily, examining it as he spoke. "Why then, Mason? Why now, Mason?"

Mason's limbs felt like ice. The bile still burned his throat and threatened to erupt. He looked over his shoulder. Rae stood a half-step behind him. The boy and his wreck of a father at her side. Mason's eyes fell to his feet.

"Hey!" Bailey's voice cracked like a whip. "I asked you a question. It's impolite not to pay attention when someone is speaking to you. Why do I see… you! Spit flew from his mouth like a ravenous dog.

"Why, why, why?"

He started to mutter and chuckle nonsensically to himself.

Rae stepped forward, calm, eyes like cut glass. "We're just passing through."

Bailey's grin widened. "A nigger bitch, Mason? Really?"

Mason stood silently. His face burned.

Bailey rubbed his own eye with the fistful of dirt, then flung it at Mason.

Mason turned his head without moving as the dirt hit him.

Rae took a step back.

Bailey laughed with his mouth closed, then froze with both arms at his sides.

"Why did you bring me niggers, Mason? Surely these aren't your friends?" He said the word friends like it tasted bad.

Mason couldn't speak. Words flew through his head, but he couldn't wrangle any of them enough to get them out.

His old life—the poison of it—seeped into his lungs.

The boy shrank behind his father. Bailey ran over and hunched down, trying to stare at the boy as if inspecting him.

"Little boy," he said, peering around the father's legs as the boy hid.

"He's just a baby monkey," he said as he tilted his head.

Bailey snapped straight and walked away from the boy and his father. "God's cleansing the Earth, Mason." He turned to look at the father.

Rae stepped forward. "This faggot got a death wish, Mason?"

Bailey took a step—and without warning—pulled the gun out and shot the father point-blank in the head.

The man's head snapped back and his body went limp.

The boy screamed — a raw, piercing sound. He gripped his father's pants at the waist to keep him standing. For a second, he struggled with the weight before it became too much. He let go, and his father's body slumped to the ground.

Rae sprang forward, but two of Bailey's men caught her mid-air. They pinned her arms and throat as she thrashed wildly, limbs moving in all directions.

Bailey leveled the gun at her. "I don't wish death, I deal it, nigger."

"Fuck you, motherfucker."

"Rae!" Mason choked. His heart hammered like it wanted out of his ribs.

Frozen solid, he stood and watched. His hand shook uncontrollably. Tiny static shocks lit up his tongue.

Rae turned her head, struggling. "Mason—" The man's hands still locked around her throat muffled her voice.

Bailey turned the pistol toward Mason before turning it back to his own head. He tapped his head repeatedly with the tip of the gun.

"Why can't parents teach their fucking kids to be quiet when adults are talking?" The end of his question came out as a desperate scream. Bailey dropped his arm and scrambled back over to the boy, kneeling and putting his face right next to the boy's ear.

The boy squirmed away, trying to put distance between the two of them.

"Shut the fuck up, you little monkey," Bailey screamed. Veins on his face and neck bulged out from the force of his words.

Bailey stood and carelessly strolled back to stand in front of Mason.

"Are you with us, Brother? You should be. God's watching." Bailey tilted his head like a lost puppy.

Everything slowed. Sound became a smear. Like the world was underwater.

Mason's hand moved. Reflex. His fingers brushed the knife on his hip.

That old self was screaming to come back and preserve Mason's safety.

His role in this gang—his obedience—his shame, the cowardice, the filth, all the poison inside him surged to the surface.

But there was something else inside him rising, too.

In the chaos, his eyes flicked up and behind Bailey. Twenty-five yards away, a monster sniffed around the trash on the back of the strip mall, as if in slow motion, quietly pawing its claws across the glimmer of a trash bag—searching for shine.

He gripped the blade. When he spoke, his voice was steady.

"Let me do it," he said.

"And what would that be, brother?" Bailey asked, locking eyes with him.

"Kill her," Mason said. "God is watching, Brother." And for once, Mason hoped that was true.

Rae's face contorted. "Mason?! What the fuck, dude?"

Bailey clapped his hands with the pistol and machete. The man was giddy. It made Mason's stomach turn.

Bailey danced in a circle of crazy kicking up dust, then paused, looking both amused and suspicious. "You're serious, Mason? I don't like fibs, Mason."

He shouted again, spit flying from his mouth. "You know I don't like fibs!" His wild eyes locked onto Mason. He breathed hard.

Mason lifted his shirt, exposing the faded swastika ink scarred across his stomach.

"I can see you, Brother," Mason said, voice trembling.

Bailey laughed. "Is that right?" he asked, his eyes narrowing. "Alright then. Do it."

The gang chuckled in unison. One of the others chimed in. "Fuck that. Make him kill the boy."

The boy looked up from his place at his father's body. He said nothing, but his body trembled.

Rae screamed again. "Mason!" Disbelief, anger, and shock all filled the sound.

"Beautiful. Just beautiful. You see, we are the celestial. We are gods, Mason! We, us, me, you!" Bailey pointed at himself and others with the gun and machete.

"Go ahead, Mason. Go, go, go!" Bailey's voice was full of amusement.

"Fine," Mason said. He wiped the smudges from the blade onto his jeans.

Mason tipped his head to Bailey and walked to the boy.

Rae screamed, "Mason, what the fuck is wrong with you?!" Her voice cracked at the end.

He didn't look at her. He couldn't.

The boy stood and tried to run. Mason pounced on him,

grabbing the boy by the arm and pulling him back. He did his best to ignore the pain surging through his body and mind while the boy fought against him.

Bailey giggled as he moved closer to the boy and Mason.

"No, please, no, please," the boy said through a steady flood of tears. Mason only thought he felt like a piece of shit until this moment. His stomach twisted.

He kneeled down behind the boy, and tightly wrapped an arm around his chest.

The boy stopped fighting and looked at Bailey. His body slumped a little in Mason's arms—like he was resigned to his fate.

Mason whispered into the child's ear.

"Discipline your fear. Discipline it."

The boy squeezed his eyes shut. His body shook again.

Bailey dropped into a squat, watching closely as Mason positioned the knife at the boy's throat. Bailey always got in close for a better view when he had mason do some unhinged shit to prove his loyalty. This show would hopefully be different, though.

Mason then angled his knife up toward the sunlight. The bright reflection shone like a beacon. It caught the attention of the creature in the trash. The thing jerked when the light caught. Mason was the only one who noticed when it began moving toward them, building speed as it approached.

Mason brought his mouth close to the boy's ear. "Hold on, kid," he whispered.

He aimed the reflection at the monster's eyes. The monster blindly launched itself—and landed on one of the gang members, smashing his chest to the asphalt and gnawing at the back of his skull, unable to crush it.

Chaos erupted.

Bailey turned wildly towards Rae, who had grabbed the other gang member by the back of his head and started jumping with knees to his face, shattering his nose and sending blood flying with each landing of her knee to his skull.

Bailey turned back toward Mason—confused, enraged.

"You fucking—?"

Mason pounced. He plunged the knife into Bailey's skull through the bottom of his jaw and twisted hard.

He brought his mouth close to Bailey's ears, just like he'd done with the boy seconds ago.

"For the brotherhood," he whispered as Bailey collapsed. The boy rushed back to his father's side.

Mason reached down and pried the gun from Bailey's convulsing hand. He shot the monster twice.

The creature's body fell on top of the mutilated gang member. The man, pinned under the creature, moaned pitifully as life faded from his hateful eyes. It was a fitting end.

Rae broke from the scuffle. The gang member stopped and looked at Mason as he held the pistol. Mason aimed and fired. One shot went into the man's chest. Mason squeezed the trigger again.

Click

He squeezed again, slower.

Click

The gang member fell back. But Mason didn't stop.

Click

Click

Mason continued pulling the trigger.

Rae walked to him. He didn't stop squeezing.

Click

Click

She grabbed Mason's forearm, forcing him to lower the gun.

He didn't look at her. His eyes filled with tears.

"Fuck you, Bailey," he screamed. "Fuck all of you, you piece of shit motherfuckers." His voice was raw—strained. He spat at the bodies. "Fuck your hate. Fuck your power. Fuck your head games. Fuck your brotherhood!"

She put one hand on his shoulder.

"Mason," was all she said.

She slowly grabbed the pistol and lowered his arm as the empty pistol's hammer fell.

Mason fell silent. He wiped at his face with his sleeve.

Bodies covered the ground. The boy was still weeping over his father. Rae's entire body shook as she stood next to him. Or was it his?

Mason examined his hands, his arms, then his legs. He was covered in blood—some his, some theirs, some alien.

He still couldn't look Rae in the eyes. But after a second, she forced eye contact with him.

"You came back," she said. There was no question in her tone.

Mason swallowed hard and nodded. "Yeah, I did," he said.

"I was worried for a second," she admitted.

He breathed out slowly.

"So was I."

Chapter 9

The three of them—Rae, Mason, and the boy—headed deeper into the city, searching for shelter as night fell. No one spoke.

The city didn't either. It just groaned under its own corpse weight, buildings sagging like exhausted giants. The boy clung to Rae's hand, sobbing in quiet, broken loops. A sound like someone replaying trauma on repeat with no pause button. Over the last 72 hours, the boy had lost everyone.

Mason was stunned the boy was able to leave his father's corpse behind. The kid must have known his father was gone before he was killed — the boy seemed smart enough. As smart as any young man could be, given the scenario he was in.

Rae covered his father with an old tarp before they left and spoke some quiet words to the boy. Mason wanted to hear, if only to steal some hope for the next leg of the journey. But he gave them space.

All the boy did was cry and walk.

Mason didn't look at the boy, unsure if eye contact would comfort the young man or drive him to kill Mason for ever being associated with a man like Bailey—if he even was a man.

Rae kept looking back at Mason as they walked. It made him feel like he was an unknown variable to their very survival.

Mason kept quiet; knife still blood-wet, replaying every second of what he'd done. Redemption didn't feel like heroism. It felt like guilt wearing a medal.

The sun dwindled. Shadows stretched long and thin behind them.

They passed many survivors — stragglers, scavengers, casualties still breathing. Two alien beasts gnawed on something no one wanted identified. They stuck to back alleys, hugging the dark like a second skin, allowing Rae to call their movements at every open area and split in the road.

When they approached an old loading dock, they froze.

Rae turned to Mason. "Night is falling. They may get active soon."

Mason nodded. "What's the move?"

"See that loading dock?" Rae pointed.

There were people. A group of them: ten, maybe fourteen.

"Okay…so you actually want to link up with them?" Mason asked. Their experiences with extra people so far hadn't been stellar. He wasn't sure how he felt about an entire crew of them.

"I do," Rae said, "but first maybe you should look to see if you recognize any of them from prison before they see us."

A smart-ass smile played across her lips. He dropped his head.

"Yeah, okay, okay, fair point." He peeked out again.

"No," he said. "No one I recognize."

It was a mixed mess of humanity—housewives with eyes rubbed raw, kids with dirt-streaked cheeks, working-class men gripping pipes and makeshift weapons like they were trying to hold on to normality by the handle.

"Okay, I'll go first. Then you and the boy follow," Rae said.

They all flinched when Rae and Mason emerged.

Strangers were threats now—sometimes worse than the

creatures. After all the shit he'd seen, Mason couldn't blame anyone for being paranoid.

One man lifted a crowbar. "Easy, folks. We're armed here. And not afraid to shoot." Mason doubted that was true.

Rae just raised her hands slowly. "We're passing through. We have a child with us. I understand your caution, but we've got no ill intent. We're injured."

The boy sniffled from his hiding place behind Rae's back.

A different man stepped forward—broad shoulders, hands trembling. Mason knew fear disguised as courage when he saw it, and it was written all over the man.

"We're heading to the marina," he said. "Got boats there. Word is the military secured an island offshore. Safe zone set up. Evac underway."

Mason's jaw flexed. He looked at Rae. Both of them silently agreed.

Rae called back to the man, "We just came from that direction. And it wasn't salvation. It was no different from the rest of the city."

"Assuming you're inviting us," she continued, "I have to tell you we're not going back west. We barely made it out."

The man didn't argue—he just swallowed hard.

Rae asked, "What about East? I've got family in that direction."

A woman stepped forward—thin, eyes glassy, like she'd been crying for days straight. A child clung to her leg.

"Death," she whispered. "There's only death in that direction."

No one contradicted her.

The man at the door locked eyes with Mason. The man took him in, his eyes lingering on Mason's bloody clothes before he spoke. "You gonna cause trouble, son?"

Mason was already spent. He didn't have the energy to argue.

"I don't think my crippled ass would fare well in a scuffle," he said, raising his mangled hand.

The man nodded. "It'll be dark soon. You can stay with us, but hurry and get in. We need to lock this place down."

Rae nodded at Mason and led the way through the bay doors. The wind carried distant shrieks—the beasts calling to one another.

Night fell fast. The group ushered Rae, Mason, and the boy deeper into their shelter—an old storage facility barricaded with pallets and metal shelves.

Battery-powered lamps glowed dimly. A small fire in the middle of the warehouse burned, fueled by cardboard boxes and broken furniture. The burning lacquer on the chairs left a sour taste in the air, but covered the smell of Mason's rotting hand. People huddled together like matches in a box, praying not to be struck.

After the group checked the barricades and settled the other kids, Rae and Mason sat beside the boy. Near the fire pit, a small group of men with makeshift weapons discussed sleeping and guard shifts while the rest of the group attempted to sleep.

The boy was still silent. Rae put a hand on the back of his head.

"We need to get to my brother's place," she said for the thousandth time.

Mason threw a hand in the air. "You keep saying that. What's so important about your brother's place? It is just supplies? Because I'm sure we can find those anywhere."

Rae inhaled deeply—a tremor in her breath. "It's more than that," she said. "It's his plan."

"What plan? Who plans for this?"

"He was a Ranger. Tenth Mountain Division. Better than me in everything except humility," she smiled to herself. "He's always talked about a bug-out plan. An evacuation route. A rendezvous point. Supplies, maps, comms—everything in case the world fell apart. He's always told me it's not if it all falls apart, it's when. And he's been ready for a long time now."

Mason raised an eyebrow. "And is there a safe way to get there? The tunnels were great and all, but I'm a little claustrophobic now. I'm sure you understand."

Rae's shoulders shook slightly. "Yeah, don't worry. We all are. We can get there."

"He made me memorize all the locations and all the ways to get there," Rae said. "He said if shit ever hit the fan—really hit it—his place was the gateway. People would meet there. They'd move on as a defensive group to the real safe house."

"That's the plan?" Mason asked.

"That's the plan," she said with a nod. But the crack in her voice gave her away. She wasn't as certain as she seemed.

Before Mason could respond, a small voice—thin, shaky, full of the kind of pain that ages a child ten years in one night—broke the silence.

"I know what's east," the boy said. "Dad told me our house was east."

They turned to face him. His eyes were empty. The poor kid didn't even look traumatized anymore—just hollow. He had the look of someone reality had betrayed too many times.

"They took my mom," he whispered. "And my little brother."

No one spoke.

"Not the little ones like we saw earlier. There are different ones back there."

"Different monsters?" Rae asked.

The boy's voice trembled. "Worse ones. They walk on their back legs like humans, and they are bigger, like horses. They're smart, too. They came through the windows. They... they grabbed my mom first. She screamed so loud... so loud I thought my ears broke. They didn't want her to make noise."

Rae's hand covered his. He didn't seem to notice.

"They grabbed my brother next," he said. "They like shiny things. And they don't like noise. His... his toy cop car..." The boy's face twisted in agony. "It had lots of lights. And it was loud. He loved it. It wouldn't turn off, though..." He trailed off.

Silence soaked the room like spilled oil.

The boy's sobs returned—but now quieter, deeper, and resigned.

Mason exhaled slowly. This kid was already living with ghosts.

Rae stood and lifted the boy in her arms. Her hand rested on the back of his head. It was like she was cradling a baby—not a kid more than half her height.

"I'm gonna lay him down. I'll be back," she said as she walked toward some empty shelves. Mason watched as she laid the boy on a makeshift bed.

"He's right," a man said to Mason from across the fire pit.

"About what?" Mason replied.

"The monsters are different," another man said.

"You know," Mason said. He threw his arms up. "I was thinking the ones we've seen are just not big enough. I was really hoping we'd run into something much worse."

"They're not just bigger," the man said.

"They're smarter. They're almost like hunters. They track. They pick off the weak. They're dangerous.

Mason swallowed. "Fuck me. Hunters? What the fuck?"

Rae stepped back into the circle beside Mason. He looked up at her.

"Are you hearing this shit?"

"Yeah," she said with an exhale.

"So, what do we do?" he asked.

"We move as a group," Rae said. She said it like it was the most obvious thing in the world.

"West is a dead zone, but if we move East as a unit, we can make it. Both directions are dangerous, but one direction has an end-game. There's nothing west for any of us. We know that. But East, we have hope. And numbers."

The women in the group didn't look at her.

"At the very least," Rae added, "we have a supply house. I'm telling you guys that Marina is fucked. Aliens are dropping into the water. There is no secure island. No land is safe, and those boats aren't going anywhere. All that shit you heard was just a rumor. There's no truth behind it. If these things really are smarter, then we need to be tactical, and more people equals better protection. It's that simple."

Some of the men nodded in agreement, but most of them kept quiet and avoided eye contact. She wasn't convincing them.

Mason looked at Rae. "Well, I was gonna go shopping for a new hoodie, but fuck it. I'm with you. You saved my ass and got me this far. Might as well go the distance."

She smiled at him. "Same," was all she said.

She turned to the others, waiting for a response. The silence lasted for what felt like an hour.

She finally stood. Her shadow stretched across the space like a verdict. They weren't saying no, so she made the call.

"It's settled then," she said, voice sharp as steel. "We go east to my brother's."

She met his eyes—tired, determined, broken, but standing anyway.

"We can make it," she said. "If my brothers alive, he's the only person left with a plan. And if he's dead…"

She trailed off as she looked toward the black horizon full of teeth.

"…then his house is the closest thing to salvation we've got."

There was no argument.

The survivors nodded, their silence a mix of fear and nervousness.

It was a fragile agreement. Mason had little hope it would last the night.

He stepped away with Rae. When they were out of earshot, he whispered to her.

"They aren't following us, are they?"

She shook her head. "Not a chance in Hell."

The boys' story hadn't helped. But these people were scared before the kid ever spoke. Mason wasn't excited to meet whatever creatures had left the whole group so shaken.

"Actually, I think I know why they won't come with us," he said, holding back a grin.

"Please, enlighten me," she said with a sigh.

"Well, look at them. This is a pretty pale group. Accents. Real small town vibes. And…" he gestured toward her. "You're black. I hate to point fingers…"

"You can't point many," she added dryly.

"Ouch, Rae. That hurts. Anyway, it's obviously because you're black. Black and scary."

Rae punched him in the arm. "You racist prick.," she said with a shake of her head.

They both laughed. It was a slight relief.

Later, after more of the group had settled in for the night, Rae offered to take the first watch. Mason knew without asking that she meant watching the survivors, not watching for monsters.

"Sold," Mason said, walking past her and laying at the feet of the shelving unit by the boy.

She sat down next to him and faced the group, her eyes, and probably ears, locked on the other survivors gathered around the fire.

Mason pulled out a pen and a scrap of paper he'd found.

"What are you doing?" Rae asked him.

"Writing my last will and testament," he quipped. "Trying to figure out who to leave my estate to."

She rolled her eyes at him and turned back to face the fire.

"Real quick," he continued, "is *Cold Ass Bitch* your full name, or just what you go by?"

Chapter 10

Morning crept into the storage facility like a sick truth.

Mason, Rae, and the boy readied themselves for the trip. Mason wiped dried blood from his knife and retied his leather boots.

Rae adjusted the straps on the little backpack she'd found and stuffed with pilfered supplies the night before. The boy clung to her sleeve.

They approached the rest of the group.

"If we're going to leave, we need to do it soon," Rae said to one man.

"We can't," the man said, lowering his head. Half of the group behind him had folded inward like collapsing tents. The men shifted from foot to foot.

The children cried while the women shook their heads.

"We're not going East," one said. "I can't. I won't. My kids will die out there."

Another clutched her teenage son to her chest. "No. No more walking," said to everyone. "No more fighting. We're not going anywhere. We're staying here and waiting for help. We're safe enough here."

Another woman started to argue with her, while a third

seemed to root down with her. Whispered bickering took hold of the group.

Fear had turned their limbs to stone. People think fear makes you run. It doesn't. Sometimes it roots you to the ground like a gravestone waiting for a name.

Rae spoke up. "Okay," she said with a solemn nod. "We understand. But we're still going. We wish you all the best," she told them.

She raised her hand. The man looked at her and shook it.

"Watch your blind corners," she said.

"Be safe out there," he replied.

Mason stood a few feet away. He talked to the boy—a mostly one-sided conversation where he tried to comfort the kid.

When he looked up, he saw Rae glance over at him. Another man from the group pulled her aside.

"Yeah?" Rae said to him. "What's up?"

"I don't know your story but that fella you're with—you just be careful. He's got the looks of a skinhead. I don't like to judge, but where I come from, those are dangerous folk to tie yourself to. Especially since…"

The rest of the man's sentence fell off.

Mason rolled his eyes. This shit again. The man's warning bothered him more than it should have. More than it usually did when people judged him. Rae didn't need saving. This fucking idiot had no idea who he was talking to.

Rae nodded, and Mason waited.

"Yeah," she said with a chuckle. "He gets that all the time. Funny thing is, he's actually just super gay. Loves dudes. Can't get enough of 'em." She patted the man on the shoulder and gave him a shrug.

The man blanched at her response. So naturally, she had

more to say. Mason held in a laugh.

"Turns out the brotherhood gave the best head in prison, so he had to commit."

It was then that she turned back to Mason. The two locked eyes.

"What the fuck, Rae?" he mouthed, his good hand propped on his hip to give it a little flair.

She was smiling as she walked back to him and the boy. "Let's go, you two," she said. Her voice was almost back to its usual cool tone.

"So, they're not coming with us because I look like a fucking Nazi?" Mason asked when she was closer.

"Actually, they said skinhead. Don't be a drama queen."

"That's the same thing," Mason replied.

"Maybe," she said. "Either way, it kills your stupid-ass theory."

"That's crazy," Mason said. "I really thought it was because you're black."

She shook her head. "You're such a dipshit. In all seriousness, I think it's because they're scared."

"...of you? Because of the whole black thing?" Mason cracked a small smile.

"I will break your good leg," she said, but she was grinning too.

"I've seen this on fresh soldiers on the battlefield," she said, looking back at the group. "First time in the real shit, and they freeze solid. There's no moving them. These guys are just like that. Same looks in their eyes. I want to help them. To convince them to come with us, but they won't fucking listen."

"Yeah, new guys in prison freeze like that, too. Can't figure out how to stand, let alone move. It's like their brains lock up. Too much terror—no room for decisions." He shrugged before adding, "Maybe these guys have been too comfortable for too long. That kind of life can be a casket when the shit really hits the fan. And I'd say that's where we're at currently. If these guys are done for, it's not your fault, Rae. Or your responsibility."

He scratched at the bandage on his hand while he said this. The smell wafted up to him. It was getting worse. He shifted it away from Rae, hoping to stop her from catching a whiff. She was already distracted by her savior complex; he didn't need to add any fuel to that fire.

He also didn't want any pity. He just wanted to keep going. Get somewhere safe and take a fucking breath.

Luckily, the boy was there to distract her as well. Rae kneeled down in front of him. It was like Mason was watching her transfer all of her savior energy back into a more productive cause. She brushed the kid's cheek with her thumb, then straightened his sleeves. Pointless since his clothes were filthy, but the gesture was probably comforting.

"Hey," she whispered. "We're going. Just us three now. You hear me? We'll make it."

The boy nodded—just barely. He was looking at her, but Mason could tell he wasn't seeing anything.

Heat rose up in his chest for a minute. How many times had his own mother said some shit like that?

"Everything's gonna be fine, my love."

"Mommy's all better now."

"It's all gonna be different from now on."

It was all the same bullshit in a different package, and it was always a lie. He wanted to scream at Rae for lying to the kid.

Just cut the shit, Rae, he thought to himself. Tell him the truth. He already knows everything's fucked.

Mason could see it in the kid's blank eyes, clear as day. He swallowed hard and bit back the words, though. Rae wasn't his mother. And she wasn't hurting the kid—the world was. Rae was just doing her damnedest to mitigate the damage. He couldn't fault her for that. Not after everything she'd shown him. The boy was right to trust her, just like Mason was. Because even if it all went south, it wouldn't be because she didn't give it everything she had. It sure as hell wouldn't be because she didn't care.

In that moment, he felt something like love blossoming for Rae. Not romantic love, but love for who she was. Respect maybe. Going with her wasn't just the right choice; it was the only one that made sense. Somehow, the whole world had fallen apart, and he'd ended up fighting through it with an actual hero—the kind of person he'd given up thinking could be real a long time ago. The kind of person he gave up trying to be even longer ago.

Rae stood then, and Mason shook all the sappy shit out of his head as Rae grabbed her makeshift weapon.

"The sun's rising," she said. "Let's go."
Mason looked at the sky again. Whatever god was in charge of all this had a fucked-up way of talking to people.
"Keep watching, asshole," he muttered as he walked. "I'll surprise you yet."

The three of them walked for hours. Through dead streets that reeked of rot and burned chemicals. Past cars filled with the husks of families. Past windows shattered outward.
Past claw marks on walls, doors ripped off hinges, blood dried in rust-colored rivers.

Chaos in the distance slowly danced as if waiting for someone else to step in. Eventually, they reached the old gas station. A few blocks from her brother's place, she told them as they rounded the corner.

That's where it happened. A shadow detached itself from the wreckage.

It walked on its hind legs. Its movements were deliberate. Its eyes, dead as it stared at the group.

The boy gasped. "A hunter-beast—its one of them," he said. "That's what took my mother."

Its chest heaved like a flesh balloon, its muscles spasmed as flies landed all over its body. It looked like a puppet walking itself into a nightmare. Its head was low, and its shoulders rolled forward.

Its claws manipulated objects on the ground like it was clearing the path to its prey without trying to spook them.

Rae scanned the area for an escape.

"The garage—move."

She scooped up the boy and sprinted. Mason trailed behind, fear driving his rapid limp.

The creature charged.

They dove into the open bay garage door and cut to the left toward the closed bay.

The beast followed, shrieking, its voice like metal screaming against metal.

The beast smashed into the low-hung garage door, knocking it off the rollers and flinging a cloud of dust into the air.

Its feet slid on the smooth garage floor, and it careened into a wall of tire installation equipment. It couldn't keep its balance as Mason and the others jolted in the opposite direction.

Inside the garage, tools and heavy industrial tire equipment lay everywhere—rusted wrenches, drills, massive presses, and wheeled toolboxes. Rae grabbed a pry bar and stopped to turn and face the creature. Mason grabbed a long metal pipe used to tighten down semi-truck straps.

The boy tucked himself back into the corner, eyeing the monster and possibly an escape route.

The beast rose to its feet. He must have been ten feet tall; his hand reached up to balance himself on a raised car lift.

"Rae," Mason breathed heavily. "What's the move?"

"Go for the joints," she said, circling around to the creature's blind side.

The beast let out a deep breath. A stench like a porta-potty on a sweltering day filled the air, choking them.

Mason let out a groan, covering his face over his coughs. "Aww, fuck, Rae," he said.

"Discipline it, Mason," she said.

Mason breathed in deep and let out a slow exhale. The way he'd watched her do so many times over the last couple of days.

"Okay," he said. "I've got your back. But this is gonna suck."

She locked eyes with him. "I know you do," she said. "And it's difficult being a hero." She gave him a brief smile before turning back to face the beast.

It lurched for the boy—Rae intercepted it, smashing the crowbar across its ankles. Kicking its leg out, the beast stumbled and swung its claws wildly at Rae, missing by inches. The beast pivoted and closed the distance. It caught Rae in the chest, throwing her across the room. She slammed into a tool chest so hard the drawers burst open, metal tools and parts spilling everywhere. Rae collapsed, unconscious.

Mason roared into action, swinging the bar into the creature's ribs. Bone cracked. The beast shrieked, spinning on him with feral intent.

Mason swung again, aiming for a joint on the backward-facing kneecap this time and making firm contact. The crack brought the creature to its knees.

He swung again, but the creature caught the bar mid-swing.

Its grip closed around the metal and Mason's forearm in the same motion. With a guttural jerk, it yanked him off his feet and slammed him back into the ground. He hit hard, shoulder-first, and felt something tear deep in the joint as his good arm wrenched out of its socket.

Before he could scream, the beast planted a clawed, hoof-like hand between his shoulder blades and drove him into the concrete.

The impact forced the air from his lungs in a wet burst. Mason's mouth opened, but nothing came out at first—just a strangled wheeze as the creature's weight pinned him down.

Then the pain caught up.

Mason screamed.

Mason shoved the bandage into his mouth, clamped down with his teeth, and tore it free.

White-hot pain flared as the stumps of his fingers were exposed—raw, swollen nubs and a trembling thumb on the only arm he had left that still worked. He didn't give himself time to think. He grabbed the knife and drove it down again and again into the creature's forearm, hacking like he was trying to carve the world apart—every bad choice, every failure, every reason he'd ever deserved this.

The blade bit. The monster didn't care.

It wrapped a clawed grip around Mason's torso and hurled him across the room. He slammed into the wall spine-first, bounced, and hit the floor hard, sliding through a sheen of oily runoff.

Before he could roll, the creature was on him.

It pinned him chest-first to the concrete, all its weight bearing down. Mason's lungs compressed uselessly beneath it. His breath left him in a choked gasp.

The beast's jaws opened—too wide, wrong in a way his brain couldn't reconcile—and clamped down on the back of his skull.

Pain detonated. Claws dug into his ribs. Something tore. Something else shifted where it shouldn't have. Blood poured down his face, flooding his eyes, hot and blinding. His vision burst into static.

He screamed—or thought he did. Sound didn't seem to exist anymore. There was only pressure and tearing and the certainty that this was it.

Somewhere nearby, the boy screamed.

Rae lay motionless.

Mason watched as the boy caught a glimpse of something. He ran toward an overturned toolbox and bent down to pick it up. His eyes were too full of blood—his brain too foggy—to see what it was.

The boy turned with shaking hands and pointed at the thing. As he watched the flash from the object, Mason snapped back in. The boy had a gun. He'd fired at the creature. The shot went wild—but was close enough to piss the thing off. And draw his attention.

It released its claws from Mason's body — but not his head.

It clamped down harder, dragging Mason on all fours with Mason's head squeezed in its jaws dragging him limp legs and arms across the floor streaking blood like a dirty mop, then grabbed the boy and slammed him into the wall, pinning him by the torso.

Mason dangled on his knees, hanging from the beast's mouth. The monster's breath was hot and musty, its saliva mixing with Mason's blood. The parts of the world he could see through the mix of liquids running in his eyes were spinning wildly. He tried to focus on something—anything. His eyes landed on the pistol near his bad hand. For just a moment, everything slowed.

He looked up toward the boy — small, terrified, pinned by a monster that wanted to rip him in half.

He looked at Rae — the hero he wished he'd been— unconscious and bleeding.

It was then that Mason understood.

All the shit in his life. All the drugs, the heroes he worshiped, all his failures and anxieties.

The years in prison. The brotherhood. His miserable life and his unwavering cowardice.

The choices he made. The choices he hadn't made.

Everything he'd hated about himself—all of it finally washed away. None of it mattered anymore. Some of it never did.

A warmth filled him. Not peace, but clarity. The simple choice, and the hard one. Like Rae said.

For the first time in his entire life, he knew exactly what he needed to do. And for the first time, he knew without a doubt it was the right thing.

Maybe he could be a hero after all.

He picked up the gun. His thumb pressed on the trigger guard, three nubs rested against the cylinder, and a lonely pinky held the back side of the pistol grip. With the last bits of strength he could muster, he tried to raise the pistol up over his head, but the angle wasn't right for a kill shot. He knew it wouldn't work. And time was running out.

He let out a scream. It wasn't the pathetic cry of days before.

This was a decision.

He put the barrel into his mouth, aiming it upward. The bullet would go through his skull and into the creature's head above him.

As he closed his eyes, he didn't hold back the stream of tears that came. He let them flow, and he pulled the trigger.

The bullet ripped through Mason's skull, and the world as he knew it went black.

Epilogue

The boy's name was Aaron. He'd told Rae that over breakfast. The two of them shared an MRE as they sat at her brother's kitchen table. He was nowhere to be found—not yet—but Rae hoped he would show. And if he didn't, they had enough supplies to get to the next location in his plan.

Aaron stared at the ring on the table between them.

"It was his," she said, tilting her chin toward the garage where Mason's body still lay. It wasn't a fitting memorial. He deserved better. But getting eaten by one of those hulked-out monsters wasn't exactly a tribute to his sacrifice either.

Rae had still been unconscious when Mason did it. By the time she came to, Aaron was in her face, shaking her by the shoulders and screaming at her to wake up.

"Rae! Rae wake up! Mason—Mason—"

She groaned, blinked, pain pulling her face tight.

"He… he shot himself. Through his head. And it… it killed the monster. It killed it." He was screaming. His voice was a mix of disbelief and shock.

Rae dragged herself over to Mason's body. She stayed next to him for a minute or two. She couldn't bring herself to believe what she saw. The knot sat tight in her throat. She couldn't breathe. There was an ache in her chest that was too deep to be from her physical injuries. She felt hollow. Her throat squeezed.

Rae reached over then and fished in Mason's pockets. She wanted something—anything — to remember him by. Not that she could forget him, but having something from him just felt necessary.

In the first pocket, she found a small, crumpled piece of paper. She stuffed it in her own pocket without looking at it. Then she found the ring. It was simple: a shiny, broken band with a small streak of gold that filled the broken place. She'd seen him wearing it before he lost his fingers, but it wasn't until she held it in her hand that she realized it was a Kintsugi ring. The Japanese art of joining broken pieces with gold. Had Mason known what the ring meant? Or had he just stolen it from somewhere?

She thought of his words that first night.

"I was going to kill myself tonight," he'd said.

It had filled her with a mix of anger and pity in that moment. What a weak man. What a sad life.

But when she looked at his body that day in the garage, she didn't feel pity for him. He'd saved her. He'd saved the boy. She looked at what remained of Mason Hale and felt respect, appreciation, and maybe even love.

She didn't fully know who he used to be, but she was proud of who he'd become. And whether he knew it or not, he was the embodiment of that ring he wore. His brokenness—his imperfections—that's where the gold was.

"Crazy fucker," she whispered, a small grin emerging from the pain. "That's how you go out, huh?"

She closed his eyes with her fingertips and took the pistol from his hand. For a moment, she wrapped her fingers around his and sat quietly.

Then, she stood and took the boy's hand. Together, they made the rest of the journey to her brother's house.

And here the two of them sat at her brother's table, planning the next round of this fight. The piece of paper lay next to the ring in front of her. She hadn't opened it yet. Afraid that it said nothing, and more afraid that it might say something. She wasn't sure which would be worse.

She reached across and uncrumpled it. Mason's handwriting was as awful as she expected, but the words he wrote took her by surprise.

> *Rae,*
>
> *I thought people like you didn't exist, but I was wrong. You are brave and strong and absolutely terrifying. But you're good. And that's rare these days—a truly good person. Thank you for...*

Rae folded the note without finishing it. She swallowed back the tears that threatened to burst.

"What's it say?" Aaron asked her.

She shook her head, swallowing until she was sure her voice wouldn't betray her. Then she slipped the ring into her pocket along with Mason's note.

"It's nothing," she said. "I couldn't even read most of it. Just scribbles."

She hoped Mason felt brave at the end—hoped he felt the weight of the choice he was making.

It was the end of the road for Mason. Maybe it always had been. But thanks to him, she still had farther to go, and she'd take this road for as long as she could.